Book # 1

THE
Painting
ON THE
Pond

Happy Reading &
Best Wishes Always!

Sharon Lewis Koho

12 - 8 - 06

THE Painting ON THE Pond

BY SHARON LEWIS KOHO

BONNEVILLE BOOKS™

Springville, Utah

ISBN: 1-55517-703-4
e. 2

Published by Bonneville Books
Imprint of Cedar Fort Inc.
www.cedarfort.com

Distributed by:

Cover design by Nicole Cunningham
Cover design © 2003 by Lyle Mortimer

Printed in the United States of America
10 9 8 7 6 5 4 3 2 1

Printed on acid-free paper

Library of Congress Cataloging-in-Publication Data

Koho, Sharon Lewis, 1946-
    The painting on the pond / by Sharon Lewis Koho.
        p. cm.
    ISBN 1-55517-703-4 (pbk. : alk. paper)
1. Artists--Fiction. 2. Northwest, Pacific--Fiction. 3.
Alaska--Fiction. I. Title.

    PS3611.O37P35 2003
    813'.6--dc21

                            2003013328

Dedicated to:

BJ and Janet, Snow and Torbjorn,
Whose youth, enthusiasm, beauty, and spirit
Inspired the characters in this book.

With love and gratitude to:

Bill, DoNae, Tiffany,
Chantel, Ryk and Derek
Sandy, Doris,
Beth and Clint.

Special Appreciation to:

Kathleen M. Charlie, Geologist
Northern Regional Office, State of Alaska
DNR Division of Mining/Water Management
Bob Engelbrecht, Tempsco Helicopters, Skagway, AK
Robin Lee Hatcher
Dr. James N. Frey
and my mentor
Kieth Merrill

Special Recognition to:

BJ Koho
Ralene Patten
Dr. Betty Turner
And my Champion, Helen Swim

PART I

Chapter *1*

David Young whistled a lighthearted tune as he closed his cabin door and walked toward the barn. Stopping beside his new Jeep Wrangler he smiled, passing his hand across its finish with an air of worship. *I've waited a long time to get my hands on a honey like this*, he thought.

A few dried bird droppings on the fender caught his eye. "All right, who's the wise guy that plastered my 'wheels'?" David growled, flicking them off. The flock of sparrows in the Douglas Fir tree across the driveway ignored him. "I parked over here so you wouldn't do that," he complained, pulling his flannel shirt out of his jeans. He spat on the shirttail and wiped away the remaining specks. David buffed the vehicle's surface and stepped back admiring the apple-red shine. Then he proceeded to the barn.

While he saddled his Appaloosa, his blue-gray eyes scanned the landscape. The beauty surrounding him still seemed like a fantasy, so unbelievable, yet it was real.

Filled with a thrill of awe and excitement, David broke into a wide grin. At last his dreams could be fulfilled.

David settled his tall frame on Cochise's saddle, trotted his horse to a flower sprinkled knoll on the hill behind his cabin, and dismounted. He sat on a log, stretching his long arms, then plucked a spear of grass and tucked the tender end between his teeth.

Mountains, snow-crowned and glistening in the rising sun, towered above the rich green meadows and forests of the foothills. The morning mist climbed from the valley floor and seeped through a spattering of Indian Paintbrush and Sunflowers.

Until several months ago, David had led a humble existence

as a struggling artist, trying to succeed amid the noise and pollution of the city. Now, at twenty-seven, he was finally free to pursue his quest for success by painting this majesty created by the hand of God. The air was fresh and pungent with the scents of evergreens and wildflowers. David took a deep breath. "I love it here!" he yodeled, blending his voice with songs of birds and humming insects, claiming his right to be part of it all.

His mood was interrupted by the sound of a horse's hooves galloping up the trail. As the echo drew near, David caught a glimpse through the trees of a young woman riding a black stallion. Her long auburn hair rose and fell as her horse ran past and was swallowed by the surrounding trees. A strange sense of intrigue engulfed David. Goose bumps rose on his forearms below his rolled sleeves. He sat spellbound for a moment, then jumped to his feet with a compelling desire to meet her. He swung into the saddle and nudged Cochise with the heels of his boots.

The horse's hooves thundered against the ground as David urged him up a steep slope after the woman. Her horse had already cleared the crest of a ridge some distance ahead. When Cochise lunged over the crest, David jerked him to a halt. "W-what the . . . ?" he whispered, as a shiver slithered up his backbone. He had reached a grassy plateau that sloped southward to a farm. Directly in front of him and further to the north, a rock wall jutted skyward. Except for thick currant bushes at the base of the cliff, only Rabbit Brush, Hawthorns, and a few lodge-pole pines covered the terrain. The stallion he had followed couldn't have reached the farm, but there was no other place it could have gone; yet the horse and rider had vanished.

David sat gaping at the empty plateau. His horse whinnied, nervously pawing the ground. "Easy, Cochise," He gave the animal an unconscious pat. "Where the devil did she go?" David tapped his horse's flank, reining him in a slow wide circle on the plateau, searching for an answer. "Nothing," he muttered. Shaking his head, he pointed his mount back down the trail. "This is just too weird!"

When they reached home, David wiped Cochise down and let him out to pasture, then returned to the house. He absent-mindedly prepared breakfast, ate a few bites, and dumped the rest down the disposal. *Aw, its driving me nuts,* he thought, slamming the dishwasher shut. *I know it wasn't my imagination, but . . . I wonder if high altitude can cause hallucinations like a mirage in a desert. Heck if I know! Painting should clear my mind. Guess it's time to go to work.*

Forcing confusing questions away, David gathered his easel and paints and walked to the small woodland pond below his house. "I'll complete one more scene," he told himself, finding comfort in the sound of his own voice. "Tomorrow I'll take this batch of paintings to Jerry and pick up a few things in town." He set his paints on a boulder and rubbed the tense muscles in his neck and jaw. "Aspirin for sure," he grumbled.

David positioned his easel and gazed at the pond. The water was smooth and crystal clear. A reflection of clouds in the blue sky floated on the surface like a painting in motion.

David picked up several flat stones and skipped them across the pond, shattering the image of the clouds. The rocks dancing across the water reminded him of his father, drawing him into the shadows of his mind: shadows where he did not want to go. Shadows where he had hidden memories that always caused the hollow aching pain that was even now swelling in his chest. The tragedy was so long ago, yet it returned whenever he thought about his father. He believed the emptiness would never go away.

Douglas Young, a hard-working man, had always put his wife and son first in his life. The bond he built between himself and David was strong, their interests following like paths. David couldn't count how often they had cast useless fishing poles aside, finding more exciting things to do on their rare escapes from the city. Exploring the same musty cave at Hansen Reservoir, hiking, climbing trees, or testing their skill by skipping rocks across the water were favorite pastimes. Now those memories were only bittersweet echoes from the past.

David sighed, pushing away the sadness as he turned to his easel. He prepared his canvas and began painting. Then he smiled, recalling his thrill the first time his pebble finally leaped beyond the range of his father's stone.

The bushes on the other side of the pond rustled. David looked up expecting to see a deer, but nothing was visible. A strange sensation that someone or something was watching him sent an icy chill down his spine. He remained quiet for some time, but there were no more sounds or movements.

David shrugged off the apprehension, most likely it was jitters from his troubled morning. He returned to his painting, forcing himself to focus on his work. He relaxed as he absorbed the scene, working to capture the graceful beauty of swimming ducks and sunlight on the water.

He finished the simple painting and examined it with a critical eye. It was good, but lacked his usual depth. Placing the wet canvas in his case, he paused, disturbed by another impression that he was not alone. He looked about but saw nothing and chided himself for being so jumpy. Yet, he could not dismiss the feeling.

A loud snap echoed across the pond and something moved in the bushes. David stared. *It's just an animal*, he thought, turning toward his cabin, but the haunting presence of something unseen raised the hair on the back of his neck. He whirled about, sucking in a startled breath.

Behind the bush, like some enchanted mythical being, stood the same young woman he had seen that morning. David's heart pounded as their eyes met, then she fled into the woods. For a moment David was dazed with astonishment, then he sprang into action. "Hey wait," he yelled, sprinting around the small pond and plunging through brush and trees. He halted, gripping a branch while cold sweat from his hand moistened the bark.

The forest appeared primitive, untouched by humanity. The woman had faded into its eerie silence.

Chapter 2

David spent a restless night and welcomed the sunrise, anticipating his trip to town. Whether he had seen a mirage or a hallucination, the vision of the woman would not leave him alone. He needed a change of scenery. He wanted to see a flesh and blood friend. Besides, Jerry's cheer was always contagious.

After breakfast, David placed fifteen completed canvases in a wooden case he had constructed for transporting his work. He removed the convertible top of his Wrangler, tipped the back seat forward, and placed the case in the back. The wind whipped through his short sandy hair as the Jeep climbed toward the summit. David smiled, enjoying a sense of boyish pride. This gorgeous piece of machinery had not come easily. It was a well-earned reward for eleven years of hard work and sacrifice.

A pang of remorse pricked David as he remembered grumbling about his lot in life. Never in the presence of Jan Young, his ailing mother, of course, but he had felt very sorry for himself at times. He knew his mom had sensed his frustration. He never resented her, but her constant pain and needs were sometimes hard for one so young and so full of dreams to cope with. Yet she understood, never allowing him to let go of those dreams.

He felt ashamed, wondering how often his selfish desires had left her needs and loneliness unheeded. Here he was enjoying his good fortune and freedom while his mother was confined to that miserable wheelchair. If only she could have remained as free as her indomitable soul. David shook the thought away, refusing to feel the old anger. Nothing could change the past.

"Hey, cut the guilt trip," he told himself aloud. Coming here, buying a new rig, and moving forward with his career was his mother's idea. She had wanted it more than anything she'd ever wanted for herself. David pictured his mother in his mind, her short blond curls, pretty face, and smiling blue-gray eyes. As frail as her body was, her spirit and tenacity never diminished. David knew if he had not followed his best friend, Jerry's recommendation to transfer, his mom would have abandoned her writing and gone out to work in spite of pain and her doctor's advice. She'd nearly sold her home and moved into a facility for the handicapped just so David would be free of her care. He couldn't recall how many times he had to argue with her about that dumb idea.

David smiled and shook his head. *I've just got to succeed so I can afford the best possible care for her,* he thought. He did miss her and wished he could have brought her with him. However, Indian Valley was far too remote and even though his mother was better than she had been in years, it was too soon after her recent surgery to even consider moving her.

David reached Indian Summit and began the winding forty-mile descent through the mountains to Slater Valley. The town of Slatersville lay twenty miles further to the north at the base of Buckskin Mountain. David took a deep breath of fresh, forest air and relaxed, enjoying the drive. An hour later he reached the valley floor and accelerated toward town.

The previous summer David's art dealer, Jerry Stone had visited Slatersville during his vacation. Overwhelmed at the possibilities in the small resort with its spectacular scenery, David's impetuous friend had rented a little shop with an apartment in the rear and re-established his art gallery there. His idea was an instant success. By late January, Jerry was calling David several times a week, begging him to relocate.

By mid March, Jerry's urging and David's mother's insistence got the best of David's curiosity and adventurous spirit. Newly unleashed desire for fame and fortune burned within him. After he made arrangements for his mother's care, he had driven his father's old pickup to Slatersville.

Jerry had closed shop with the excitement of a child in wonderland and taken David on a tour of the area. Then, still bragging about his beloved region, he drove David over the winding snowy pass to Indian Valley.

Beneath rugged mountains, amid frosty hills and forests of fir and pine trees, David had spotted a for sale sign in front of a log cabin. It was nestled in a clearing surrounded by pines, aspens, chokecherry trees, and wild rosebushes. A mountain stream, still carrying shards of ice, flowed past the house and emptied into a pond seventy-five yards beyond. With a sense of excitement and reckless conviction, David purchased the cabin.

By the first of April, his affairs were in order and he had arranged full-time care for his mother. He had packed the pickup, bid her an emotional farewell, and set off for his new home in Indian Valley.

As he drove into town, David again took note of the quaint, rustic appeal of the village. Although there were modern buildings on the outskirts of Slatersville, most structures in the older township were simple one or two-story buildings connected to each other like Jerry's shop.

In deep contrast with its surrounding, an air of mystery hovered around a three-story mansion behind the art gallery. The grand estate and its spacious grounds took up more than half the block. Ivy climbed the gray-stone walls and wound around the peaked gables of the house. The stately old manor seemed out of place and distant, like part of a forgotten time from a different world. As David passed the mansion and turned in front of the art gallery, he mused that one day he should set it to canvas.

When David opened the gallery door, Jerry's black-rimmed glasses and sharp nose appeared above the counter. Jerry sprang up from the paintings he was filing, surprise and warmth lighting his dark blue eyes.

"Dave, how's it going?" Hurrying around the counter, he grabbed his friend in a rowdy hug. "I was beginning to think you got lost in those hills." He stood back grinning smugly. "You really like it here, don't you?" Without waiting for an answer he tossed his head in a cocky, know-it-all manner, and walked outside to David's Jeep. "Eh, I knew you would. What have you got for me?"

David, his mouth still open to respond, just shook his head chuckling to himself as he followed Jerry. They carried the wooden case inside, and Jerry began lining the landscape paintings against the walls. David displayed the fresh painting of the pond on the counter, then walked into Jerry's kitchen, opened the refrigerator, and helped himself to a soda.

"Wow, Dave! These are good," Jerry said admiring David's work. He ran his hand through his short, curly black hair. "How did you complete so many?"

"Hard work, bud. They didn't paint themselves. I must admit the settings are terrific." David leaned against the inner door frame of the shop as a mischievous smile spread across his face. "It's tough as ticklin' a badger decidin' which ones to paint first." Pleased with his attempt at country lingo, David strolled to an easy chair and sat down, watching Jerry work. He stretched his legs across a table strewn with art magazines and leaned back, placing his free hand behind his head while his grin broadened. "Well, pardner, I've done my share. I'll take my advance now. You'd best start framin' and sellin' so I can enjoy a life of ease and luxury." Yawning noisily, he settled deeper into the plush chair.

"Yeah, you lazy . . . I do all the work, you get all the glory. The old saying is . . . what goeth before the fall? Pride, I think." Jerry bopped David on the head. "Give up the jargon, Dave. That city-bred imitation would slay any blue-blooded cowboy."

"How would you know? At least I educate myself by watching old western re-runs." David smoothed his hair and glanced at his painting of the pond. Then, remembering the woman across the water, his face sobered. Picturing her in his mind, she seemed so real, yet . . .

"What's wrong, Dave?"

David rose and picked up the painting, staring at the place

8

she had been standing as he carried the canvas back to his chair. *The same mirage appearing twice in different locations is about as likely as a stuffed rabbit having babies,* he thought. *I wasn't hallucinating either.* He gave a deep sigh and sat down. *I have no answers, but she was really there.* Somewhere inside him, a strong witness bore truth to his thoughts.

"David, talk to me. What's wrong?"

"Huh? Oh, I'm sorry, Jerry. I guess I'm a little preoccupied. I had the strangest experience yesterday. I saw a woman, twice, yet both times . . . she just vanished."

Jerry sat in a chair across from David. "What do you mean *vanished*? Let's make some sense here."

David leaned back shaking his head. "I can't make any sense out of it, Jerry. Believe me, I've tried." Describing his two encounters with the young woman, David realized his attempts to shut them out of his mind had only been a denial of a deeply troubling phenomenon.

"Man, that's a lot to swallow. If I'd heard it from anyone but you . . ." Walking to the window, Jerry thoughtfully rubbed a faint shadow of whiskers already growing on his shaved chin. "I don't know. You've been working hard, Dave. Maybe too hard, why not just ease up for a while . . . get a little R-and-R. Unless . . . nah," he said to himself shaking his head.

"Unless what?" David leaned forward in the chair.

Jerry turned around with a nervous chuckle. "Oh, just a weird coincidence. I've heard there's a legend about a ghost who haunts this area. I guess that mansion behind my place was her home."

David stared wide-eyed at Jerry. "Don't be absurd. You know I don't buy that supernatural stuff." He paused, somehow uncertain of his own response. Then gazing at the painting again, he grew quiet, slipping deeply within his own thoughts. *This is so unsettling. I wonder who she is?*

Jerry furrowed his brow. David was not one to get carried away by imagination or fantasy. Whatever he had seen had clearly unnerved him.

Finally David stood up. "Well, I'm not swallowing any legend. I'm sure if I knew all the facts the whole thing would be perfectly sensible. I'd better head out, Jerry. I've got a lot of business to attend to."

Jerry tried to convince David to stay, but he declined. Still objecting, Jerry wrote a check and walked David to his Jeep.

David argued with himself while he attended to his business, but his curiosity and a nagging fascination about the legend finally won. He put off his grocery shopping, and drove to the public library. He felt foolish for even considering such nonsense, but he approached the elderly librarian sitting at the information desk nevertheless.

She smiled pleasantly. "What can I do for you, sir?"

"I'm new in town, and I . . . I'm kind of interested in old legends," David stammered. "I understand one originated here. Could you tell me about it?"

The gray bun of hair on the woman's head bobbed up and down as she nodded. "Oh, yes," she said trying to sound mysterious, with a storyteller's gleam of delight in her faded eyes. "Marnie's ghost." Motioning David to a chair, she folded her hands in front of her and sat up, looking important.

"About a hundred and ten years ago, a wealthy man named Jacob Slater founded this town. He was a stubborn, proud man and thought his family should be examples of the high society he wanted to bring here. His daughter, Marnie, was a sweet girl, very down to earth. She refused to get caught up in the showiness of his wealth. She fell in love with her father's stable hand, and they became secretly engaged. Her father found out and was furious. He fired the young man, and then tried to arrange Marnie's marriage to a wealthy European. She refused, embarrassing her father and making him angrier than ever.

"The stable hand knew her father would never consent to their marriage unless he had money behind his proposal. He went to Alaska to prospect for gold and finally struck it rich. He wrote to tell Marnie he was coming to get her." The librarian dropped her head, peering over the top of her glasses, and changed her voice to a low cryptic tone. "He never arrived, and

10

no one ever found any trace of him." The woman sighed.

"Marnie had gone into seclusion after he left for Alaska. She remained lonely and isolated, waiting for his return. When he disappeared, she was beside herself with grief. Then one day, after a storm, she went for a ride on her horse and didn't come home." The woman lowered her eyes, dabbing at them with a handkerchief. "They found her and the horse at the base of a cliff on Buckskin Mountain, where a ledge she was riding on had crumbled in a mud slide. Long after she was buried in the family cemetery, people insisted they had seen her wandering about the valley in search of her lost love." The woman's voice became a whisper as she cast her eyes about. "Some claim she still does."

Chapter 3

Dusk was approaching when David completed his shopping and drove by the Slater estate on his way home. As he passed, he caught a glimpse of a young woman walking into an alley between the old mansion and Jerry's apartment. His breath stuck in his throat. He slammed on his brakes, coming to a dead stop in the middle of his lane of traffic.

"That was her," he gasped, unmindful of screeching tires and a blaring horn behind him. He flipped a U-turn in the street and drove back to the alley. David leaped out of the Jeep, his heart pounding wildly in his chest. Was he losing touch with reality? Behind the restaurant adjoining Jerry's art gallery a chain link trash enclosure extended across the lane to the high board fence around the mansion. There was no shrubbery and no gate in the wooden fence, but the woman was gone.

David felt adrenaline flooding his system as he ran around the corner of the mansion toward the front gate. *I'm getting some answers right now*, he thought. He gripped the latch on the huge iron gate, but found it locked.

"Them folks is gone, Sonny," an elderly man called from his front porch across the street.

David nearly walked in front of a car as he hurried across the street. "Do you know if anyone has been there recently?" he asked the old man.

"Nope, it's been locked up like that for more'n a week. I ain't seen nobody."

"Does a young woman live there?"

"Yeah, a cute little thing with short blond hair. Haven't seen her around for some time though. Think she's been away at school. Hey, what you wanna know for?" His eyes narrowed. "You're a stranger around here ain't you?"

"Yes, I am," David answered. "I thought the person I was

12

looking for lived here, but her hair isn't blond. I must be mistaken."

I need to talk to Jerry, David thought, walking back to his Jeep. Then he stopped. *No, he'd think I was nuttier than a nut roll.* David had always seen himself as intelligent, clever, organized, good at whatever he did, and mentally strong and stable. Now he stared down the vacant alley and shook his head. "Maybe I am crazy," he mumbled.

By the time David reached the mountain pass a disturbing revelation had begun to unfold. He had seen what he had seen, and the impression following each experience had been profound. Somehow, he sensed that the woman and the mystery surrounding her was the setting for some impending trial that would challenge all of his heart and strength. He had previously felt the cold foreboding arms of fate, helplessly trapped in her chilling grasp. Now, strange encounters with no answers, the fateful legend of the ghostly Marnie Slater, and this unwelcome revelation, were unhinging his reasoning powers.

Shadows were deepening along the winding highway and dark images pressed on his mind. David felt his fear of the unknown taking control. His hands felt numb and disconnected, like they belonged to someone else. The numbness increased, spreading up his arms and throughout his body until he felt unreal, as though he were watching himself through a dream. He gripped the steering wheel with clammy fingers, battling his growing dread.

When David reached home, he threw enough hay to Cochise to quiet his impatient nickering and went to bed. However, sleep wouldn't come. David lay in the dark room trying to think of other things, but it was useless. His mind kept drawing him back into the shadows of the last two days. Again and again he attempted to push away the legend, but it seemed to hover over him like an omen. The heavy blackness crowded closer.

David sprang upright in bed and flipped on the lamp. He rose and drew a glass of water. After swallowing the cold liquid, he studied his haggard image in the bathroom mirror. "Come on man, snap out of it," he ordered aloud. "This is ridiculous. What's the matter with you? You've never let anything get to you like this before. So some gorgeous female does vanishing acts. You've got to get hold of yourself." Denying himself feelings that seemed irresponsible or resembled fear, David went back to bed, determined to get some much-needed rest, but he was still awake when the first rays of the sun peeped over the mountains.

Running his hand through his tousled hair, he yawned, got out of bed, and wearily pulled on his clothes. He trudged outside and saddled Cochise and rode to the plateau where the woman had vanished. David walked through the heavy brush, attempting to work his way toward the cliff, but found the shrubbery impassable.

"Ow," he yelled as a Canadian thistle stabbed through his jeans, piercing his skin with its needle sharp spikes. "Wherever she went, it wasn't through here, unless she is Jerry's ghost," David growled, extracting the thistle spines.

The song of a bluebird floating on a breeze reached David's ears. Larkspur, Indian Paintbrush, and a dozen varieties of wildflowers were sprinkled through the meadow grass of the plateau. The sunlight shining on David's back bathed the earth with its warmth. It was the kind of day that inspired David's greatest creative powers, but he felt no desire to paint. Instead, an odd heaviness hung over him, the former night's premonition still nagging that something dark and ominous lay ahead. Groaning aloud, David sat against the trunk of a lodge-pole pine and stared blankly at the scene before him. He hadn't felt this kind of emptiness since his father's death.

In an instant, a startling realization came to him as though gently whispered to his mind. He recalled his mother's parting words when he left her in the care of her new nurse.

"You have to go, David," she had said, smiling though her tears. "This is a great opportunity for you and Jerry. You've worked so hard for it. You're recognized as an accomplished artist now. This will give you a chance to expand your career.

I wish I had no misgivings. I think you might have some hard things to face, but deep inside I know your decision is right." Her courage had crumbled for a moment as a sob escaped her lips. "May God go with you."

She felt what I'm feeling, David thought. He stood up. *She sensed some imminent hardship, but she never tried to stop me.* With renewed strength, he took a deep breath. *I don't know what lies ahead, but coming here was the right thing to do.*

The phone was ringing when David returned home. Jerry, worried about David's state of mind, had called to check on his friend.

David was relieved to hear someone's voice instead of his own thoughts. However, fearing that Jerry would think him mad, he held back with small talk. Jerry stubbornly pressed him for more. David gave in and told Jerry about the young woman behind the Slater mansion the night before. "I know this all sounds ridiculous," he said, "but this girl is getting to me, Jerry. I couldn't even sleep last night."

"Dave why don't you spend a few days here with me? You could ease up, unwind a little, and . . . maybe you could see a doctor . . . you know, get something to calm your mind."

David sensed concern in Jerry's voice. He tried to lighten up. "Hey, I'm all right, Jerry. I just need to get some sleep. I'll call you tomorrow."

David fixed himself a sandwich and watched TV while he ate. Then, feeling the strain and fatigue of too many hours without rest, he crawled into bed and fell asleep.

In his dreams, David found himself standing beside his woodland pond. The Master Artist had created a scene of exquisite beauty surrounding the pond. Boughs of evergreens stirred in the breeze. Leaves of the aspens quivered, and chokecherry blossoms gently bowed to the reflection of the clouds floating against a deep blue sky.

As he watched, the scene was transfixed into a motionless painting on the still surface of the pond. The water became strangely iridescent. Drawn by the unusual illumination and the frozen reflections on the water, David sat on his heels. He looked at his own image on the mirror-like surface, then he stirred the water, watching myriad colors dancing on the ripples.

As the shimmering hues gathered again and settled, they formed a haunting picture. The figure of a woman with long auburn hair and a flowing white gown lay beside David's image on the water. He recognized her face. Her eyes, filled with an expression of sorrow, held David in their hypnotic gaze as she reached toward him.

"Marnie?" he whispered, falling back from the reflection of her outstretched hand. Yet, something deep within him yearned to comfort her. Unnerved, he sensed her presence on the shore beside him, close enough to touch. He could almost feel her breath on the nape of his neck. He spun about, but emptiness surrounded him with its heavy silence.

Chapter 4

David was awakened by a flock of sparrows twittering in the fir tree outside his window. Rolling over, he looked at his digital clock and groaned. "It's only five thirty, you stupid birds. Have you no mercy for a suffering man? I need to sleep in this morning." He rolled back toward the wall, pulling the pillow over his head.

A loud knock echoed on the front door. "Oh no, what now?" David grumbled, tossing the pillow across the bed and pulling on his robe. "What do you bet it's my ghost? When I answer the door, no one will be there." Tying his belt, he jerked the door open and stepped back in surprise. "Jerry, what are you doing here?"

"Gather your camping gear friend," Jerry said with a grin. "I'm taking you to the prettiest fishing spot this side of heaven. The trout can't wait to jump on your hook."

"I'm sure." David yawned, motioning Jerry to a chair. "You know that any fish big enough to eat, hates me. Why do you think Dad and I preferred spelunking in that musty old cave, while you and Mom caught our limit? We didn't like playing fool to a bunch of minnows." He walked to the couch and sprawled on his stomach, crossing his arms across the armrest. "Besides, we can't get rich wading in water with poles in our hands. Fish don't buy art."

"No sweat, tourist season doesn't get in full swing until June. We've got a week. Anyway, we can afford it. I caught a "big fish" from L.A. who's going to make us both rich. He wants me to furnish paintings for the lobbies and conference rooms in his new hotel chain. He'll host exhibits for us at his grand openings and hinted that greater things could follow."

"Well, aren't you informative?" David sat up, imagining the President and the Queen of England admiring his work.

"This could be our big break."

Jerry grinned. "That's the plan."

"Wow," David said, stepping into the bedroom to dress. "This will be great. You and I rubbing shoulders with big executives and celebrities! When did all this happen?"

"Last week. I could have told you sooner, but I'm still waiting for confirmation."

David laughed. "You'd explode if you ever had to keep a secret. I can't believe you didn't pop yesterday."

Jerry grew serious. "Yesterday didn't seem to be a good time. Anyway, that's why I'm here. I think you need to unwind a little."

David knew objecting would be futile. Once Jerry's mind was made up, his plans were carved in stone. Besides, the idea was enticing. "Is there a place to swim?"

"It's a glacier lake, too cold for swimming. Better bring your fishing pole."

David chuckled. "So you can show me up for the thousandth time? I don't think so. I like cold water. You fish, I'll swim."

While David packed, Jerry rented a horse from an outfitter down the road. The men rode their mounts up a steep trail between two mountains above Indian Valley. After several hours they passed through a clearing in the forest, and Indian Lake came into view. Its translucent turquoise water glimmered in the sunlight at the base of a sheer granite mountain that pierced deeply into the powder blue sky.

"Whew," David whistled as they rode along the shore. "No wonder you wanted to show me this place. It's magnificent."

The men tethered the horses to a highline near the shore and set up camp. Then Jerry broke out his fishing gear. He pulled on a pair of rubber waders and was soon hip deep in the lake, casting his line far out into shadowy depths.

Refusing to be haunted by nagging qualms that beset him, David pushed his apprehension about the girl away. He hadn't been swimming in ages and the water looked inviting so he slipped into swimming trunks.

"You're crazy," Jerry scoffed. "I told you it's fed off a glacier. You won't last thirty seconds in that water."

David ignored Jerry, scanning a deep pool for snags or rocks. Then, wearing a smug grin, he dove with the grace of an otter into the clear blue-green depths. The icy water struck him like a rock, seizing his lungs. He floundered back to shore, gasping for breath.

Jerry's laughter echoed off the mountain and rang across the lake.

Shivering as he wrapped himself in a towel, David glared at Jerry. He stretched out on the shore so the warm sand and sun could increase his body temperature. Then, too stubborn to admit defeat to Jerry or commit himself to the frustration and boredom of fishing, David mastered the frigid water by sitting astride a large log. Using a pole for a paddle, he sliced through the smooth surface leaving a trail of ripples reflecting the sunlight. However, even in this peaceful setting his mind could not escape his torment.

Later, as David and Jerry sat quietly by the campfire, an owl hooted nearby, and a coyote howl echoed through the night.

David had been strangely quiet and distant most of the day. Jerry made a final attempt to start a conversation, but David's responses were brief and dead-ended. Jerry's concern for his friend was increasing, but he didn't press. Maybe David would be his cheerful self after a night's rest. Jerry watched David moving the coals against the last smoldering log with his paddle pole.

"I think I'll turn in Dave," he said.

"Okay, see you in the morning."

David lingered, feeling small against the vast star-sprinkled universe. "Brrr," he said zipping up his coat as the warmth of the fire gave way to the night. Then another chill colder than the crisp mountain air crawled through him. David held his breath, sensing an unseen presence. The breeze carried a whisper so soft it might have been his own mind, yet it was clear and startling.

"Your journey will be hard, but you must not give up. You must fight to live."

David shuddered. He glanced about in search of the voice, but he knew its source was immaterial. He turned back to the fire pit and sat for a long time staring at the fading coals. Finally, he rose and walked to the lake shore, dipping water to extinguish the dying embers. He stood watching the faint glow of the crescent moon on the water. *Journey?* He thought with a helpless shrug. Then shaking his head he muttered, "What will be, will be." David poured the water into the fire pit stirring the steaming ashes then entered the tent. He zipped up his sleeping bag and stared into the darkness.

Chapter 5

The men awakened to a brisk morning, their breath sending puffs of steam into the air. While Jerry built a fire, David knelt to draw water from a nearby spring. He paused, gazing across the lake at the granite peak. Its rugged silhouette stood like a giant sentinel against the gray morning sky. As he watched, sunlight burst through the pass behind him. The lone prism, streaming rays of gold, swept down the snow patched slopes, sparkling on the mountain and shining on the water while the rest of the valley lay in shadows. Lost in the rare exquisite vision, David watched in awe, painting the scene in his mind.

"Pretty isn't it?" Jerry said, walking up and standing beside him. "The Indians called it, 'Ee wa tam na peh mei hee khu noo sa,' the lake with the sun shining on it in the morning."

The prism widened, then burst, filling the valley with sunlight. Immediately, birds took to the air. Squirrels chattered from the trees, and chipmunks scurried about stuffing their fat little cheeks.

For that inspiring moment, David relaxed, acting like the friend Jerry knew so well. Then the hard line formed again on David's jaw as he clenched his teeth. His head and shoulders drooped, and the distant expression returned to his eyes.

"All right Dave, I've been patient as long as I can stand it," Jerry said, facing his friend. "Come clean. What's really stressing you?"

David turned away with a shrug. "Nothing, just enjoying the view."

Jerry grabbed David's arm and stepped in front of him. "I figured you were just tired last night and needed to be left alone, but you've hardly said a word all morning. Your face looks as gloomy as a grave digger."

"It's okay Jerry, I'll be fine," David insisted, stepping around him.

Jerry blocked his retreat. "That's bull! You can't snow me. I know you too well. There's a lot more going on in your rock stubborn head than you'll admit. I'm not blind, you know."

David felt the heat rising under his collar. "Lay off, Jerry," he warned, stepping around him again and walking toward the campfire. "I said, I'm fine."

Jerry followed close on his heels. "The problem is you're too proud and pig-headed to admit you need help. Dave, it doesn't matter whether you're hallucinating or not. I don't care if you're crazy as a Mad Hatter. I'm here for you. Just talk to me!"

David spun around, and Jerry walked into him. David pushed him backward. "I said, leave it alone. You always think you have all the answers," he sputtered, slinging the pot of water on the ground. "Well, you're not so all fired smart because there aren't any answers."

David saw the hurt in his friend's eyes as Jerry stiffened and frowned at him. He instantly felt remorse for his anger. Jerry had a right to be disturbed. David hadn't been himself since that dumb plateau swallowed some woman and her horse, but he was too confused to talk about it. "Just leave me alone," he mumbled, and walked away.

As David disappeared into the trees, Jerry delivered a hard kick to the pot sending it clattering along the rocky shore. Then he grabbed his fishing gear and stomped toward the water.

Feeling miserable and stunned at his own behavior, David was angry with himself for his inability to control his mind and his emotions. Troubled by the haunting whispers the night before, he climbed to the top of the tallest peak forming the pass. Looking back, he could see Jerry fiercely casting for any fish unwary enough to approach his deadly hook. *Why did I lose it back there?* David thought, feeling ashamed. *Jerry was only trying to help. This is intolerable. I hate what's happening to me. I always have a handle on things . . . but now . . .*

When David finally returned to camp, Jerry had prepared breakfast. David noticed a dent in the pot that was now full of steaming hot chocolate. David was certain he'd only thrown it into the sand, but thought it better not to ask. Jerry didn't speak. He forked several fish and a stack of pancakes onto the plate from David's mess kit and passed it to him.

"Thanks Jerry," David said. "Hey bud, I'm sorry."

"You were right." Jerry shrugged his shoulders. "It's none of my business. I was out of line."

"No, I was the one out of line," David said, sitting on the log facing Jerry. "We've been through too much together for me to damage our friendship. You've always been like my brother."

"I know," Jerry said, glancing at David with a slight grin. "Brothers forever, remember?" Recalling years of kindness from David and his parents, Jerry became thoughtful. "You, Jan, and Doug were always my family." He picked up a fried fish with his fork, gazing almost reverently at it. "Man, Jan could out-fish us all, couldn't she? I can still see her prim and pretty with that silly pink hat on her blond curls, her nose in a book, and a fishing pole propped between her bare toes."

David felt the old bitterness, remembering his mother as Jerry described her. He stood up glancing across the lake, and swallowed a lump in his throat. "Yeah, she was something special." He sighed, and sat back down. "She still is."

"I'm sorry Dave, I didn't mean to bring back sad memories."

"That's okay, Jerry. You and I know hard times go with the flow of life. It's never steady or predictable." He absently poked at his pancakes with his fork. "Actually, that's what's been bothering the devil out of me lately. I can't understand what's happening to me. I guess I got angry with you because I've wondered if I was going crazy. I know moving to Indian Valley was the right thing to do. Something is brewing though. I sense it. I even heard . . . well, I don't know what to expect. It's like the weird feeling I told you I had just before the cop came to the stadium after the accident. I can't explain it any better, Jerry. That's all I know."

David took a sip of his hot chocolate and continued. "You were right; I do need a break. So let's not talk about it anymore this week. Just give me time to get my head back on straight."

Jerry was worried, but he smiled and nodded. "Just remember you're not alone in this. I'm here if you need me."

That afternoon, David was photographing a twisted tree growing through a crack in a boulder. Jerry had taken a string of fish to put in a small cooler he'd secured in a tree. Suddenly, Jerry cried out. David rushed into the woods following verbal tirades and fierce growling. As he came upon the scene, he burst into laughter.

Jerry was engaged in a desperate tug-of-war with a bear cub for his string of fish. "Let go, you stupid bear," he hollered. "You already got everything I had in the cooler!"

Sensing the danger Jerry's temper was oblivious to, David quickly regained control. "Forget it Jerry. Let him have them."

"No way," Jerry retorted. "He chewed through my rope and dumped my cooler. I tried to save one fish he hadn't eaten, and the thieving stinker bit me. While I was looking at my finger, he tried to steal these too."

"Hey, any second an angry mother bear will show up and bite off your head. Let's get out of here," David yelled, grabbing the cooler and running toward camp.

Growling louder than the bear, Jerry gave a final tug on the nylon cord, then released his afternoon catch and followed David.

"It's just a surface wound," David said as he treated Jerry's finger with the first aid kit. Jerry winced, still telling the world what he thought of the bear.

"Stop complaining," David said with a chuckle. "You've always been happiest standing in waders with a pole in your hand. Now you have an excuse to catch your limit twice in the same day."

The week passed far too quickly. Each day the sun rose in glory and hurried across the sky, sweeping the earth with its warmth. It settled behind the granite mountain each night leaving a flurry of colors fading into darkness. The final day of the vacation arrived, and two grubby men with whiskered faces reluctantly broke camp, mounted their horses, and started for home. Looking back, David and Jerry paused and made an agreement that this would be an annual event.

As Jerry proceeded down the trail, David lingered for a short time, his mind acutely aware that his return to Indian Valley may be the final curtain of an old saga. Long ago he learned that denial of feelings would not change the course of what the future held. A message whispered through a night breeze had confirmed what he already knew: somehow his life might never be the same.

Chapter 6

The next few days were uneventful and everything seemed back to normal. David's mood lightened, and he began wondering if imagination had intermingled with dreams and distorted the reality of the past two weeks. Finally, he put full blame for the disturbances on the dreams, reassuring himself that his mind was and had always remained sound.

Then one morning he awoke with a strange foreboding. His attempts to dismiss it were useless for the impression remained strong and troubling. David decided he'd rather be busy than uneasy, so he packed a lunch and rode Cochise into the mountains. He chose to paint an aspen grove nestled below a waterfall on the side of Thunder Mountain.

David set up his French easel, feeling his own smallness beneath the towering grandeur of the peak. He opened the case, and prepared to recreate the mountain's rugged majesty on canvas. As he sketched, he began soaking up his surroundings, and a creative mood developed, forcing worry into the background.

While David worked, Cochise grazed nearby on the rich green meadow grass. When the sun was high overhead, David gave a few more touches to his painting and sat back studying it with satisfaction.

He put his brush away and pulled his sandwich from the saddlebag. After lunch, he stretched out in the shade of a tree and watched clouds floating through the air like giant marshmallows. One twisted, flattening into an alligator, and chased an upside-down pig across the sky.

David smiled, remembering visions of clouds against the city skyline. His mother, lying beside him on the lawn, had often turned childish impressions into tales of dinosaurs and fire-breathing dragons. David realized it had been years since he'd taken time to relax enough to lie in the grass and watch the clouds. Now, as they drifted above him, and a bee flew lazily on a breeze, David drifted too. His eyelids fluttered then closed, and he lay sleeping in the tall grass.

Sometime later, David was awakened by a shadow passing over him and a touch against his face. He sat up with a start. Cochise whinnied, nuzzling David's ear.

"Get out of here you oversized pup," David playfully pushed the animal away. "You scared me." The horse thrust his nose into his master's chest, coaxing for the affectionate pat he knew he would receive. David smiled, patting Cochise. "You are such a baby. Besides, your timing is lousy. You wrecked a good dream." David got up and returned to his easel. Cochise followed nudging his shoulder. "Oh, go bother a porcupine." David gently flicked the horse's ear. Cochise snorted, tossed his head, and trotted away. David chuckled. "Going off to pout now? Good, I have work to do."

David squeezed several shades of oils onto his palette and began painting again. He was soon deeply involved in his creation.

Hours later, the light was fading and David was surprised to see the sun sinking in the western sky as thunderclouds formed on the horizon. *Uh-oh, time to pack up and go home,* he thought, cleaning his brush. He whistled, and Cochise trotted over to him.

The apprehension David had felt that morning had been forgotten while the young artist lost himself in his work. The foreboding returned when he saddled Cochise, secured the wet canvas in the case, and strapped the easel to the horse's side.

David rode his horse down the trail, while sunset spread its brilliant colors across the horizon. All too soon the final rays fell into twilight then darkened into night. Through the patchy clouds moving toward him, the silver-blue of the moon illuminated the path, casting shadows among trees and crags.

Rebuking himself aloud for his poor judgment of time, David fought growing anxiety as the trail descended into a ravine. A gusty wind arose, lashing at him like an angry spirit wailing through the trees.

Uncertain of his footing and spooked by the wind, Cochise stumbled along the path, snorting and balking, so David slid from his back to guide him over the rough terrain. Directly in front of them the chasm turned sharply, concealing the trail.

A sudden wild cry like a banshee, shrieking above the howl of the wind, pierced through David, chilling him to the bone. Squeals of terror echoed around him with a deafening crescendo. Instantly, David was struck from behind with a crushing blow.

Agonizing pain shot through his head as he was hurled onto the rocks. As lightning flashes exploded through the darkness, David saw a black stallion rearing above him, thrashing the air with deadly hooves. A woman sat astride the stallion. Her long hair swirled in the wind like a flame of fire as the lightning reflected its auburn glow.

A loud clap of thunder cracked through the air and resounding rumbles shook the ground beneath him as David's consciousness faded. Then he was engulfed in thick black silence.

Chapter 7

David gradually became aware of searing pain in his head. He felt the rocky ground beneath him, then sensed another presence very near. Terror swelled in his disoriented mind. He forced his eyes open. In the scattered moonlight glaring between the churning clouds, David could see a dark silhouette bending over him. He lay frozen, trying to clear his mind, while loud ringing echoed in his ears. A sudden, gripping pain shot through his head, and the moon started spinning above him with sickening motion. His vision began to fade as a groan escaped his lips.

The figure above him drew nearer, and he felt breath on his face. Panic swirling with the pain ripped sensibility from him, leaving only numb stupor. For a moment he was aware that he was being drug across the ground, then David fell again into the dark empty depths of unconsciousness.

Much later David stirred, vaguely sensing that softness beneath him had replaced the rocky ground. The ringing in his ears had subsided, but the throbbing pressure in his head was excruciating. He was surrounded by silence, but sensed he was not alone.

Straining to see clearly, David peered through darkness toward a flickering light, but he couldn't focus, and his eyelids were heavy. He struggled to hold them open, but he was too weak. "Can't . . ." he mumbled.

There was a sound of movement toward him, and David fought to hold onto consciousness. His strength failed, and he surrendered to sleep. Dreams came interwoven with real sensations. Something icy pressed against the back of his head, while a warm soothing hand moved across his forehead. He let himself drift into the soft lulling comfort of the touch. Nearby, the trickling sound of water pulled his mind to his woodland pond. A cool damp cloth was pressed gently against his face, and he imagined it was the tall grass.

He envisioned a breeze rustling through the leaves of the aspens, swaying the branches and pushing clouds across the sky. The pond, illuminated by a strange glow, appeared haunting with reflections of drifting clouds and waving trees lying motionless on its surface. The breeze ruffled David's hair but not even the slightest ripple stirred the water. He leaned over, submerging his hand and swirled the liquid mirror. The water remained calm, his likeness sharp and clear.

Then the figure of a woman lay beside his reflection like a beautiful, enchanted masterpiece, her long white gown flowing against the frozen background, her arm reaching toward David. He sensed her presence beside him on the shore "Marnie?" he gulped jerking away and spinning around, but he was alone. Looking back at the pond, David was mystified. Her image remained beside his reflection. A mask of sorrow covered her face. Her presence was overpowering, close enough to touch. David turned again, yearning to comfort her. She was standing beside him on the shore, her fingers resting on his hand like a whisper. He drew back for a moment then moved to encircle her shoulders in an embrace. His arms met nothing but a misty vapor floating upward on the breeze.

Then the pond vanished. Thick fog gathered around David, and he felt himself falling into deep heavy sleep.

Hours later, a bright light penetrated David's hypnotic slumber and urged him awake. He felt a searing pain as he turned his head away from the light and stared up at the ceiling of a large room. Something cold pressed against his scalp. Reaching up, he pushed an ice bag away. He glanced toward his feet and discovered he was lying on a brass bed. Sunshine pouring through a window warmed the bright colors of a patchwork quilt covering him.

Trying to clear his mind, David looked around the room. An antique dresser with a hand-carved mirror stood beside a free-standing wardrobe and an aged cedar chest. Sitting on a table beside his bed, along with an old-fashioned water bowl and pitcher, was a lighted coal oil lamp. As David's gaze rested on a photograph adjacent to the lamp he gave a startled gasp.

The black and white portrait of a family had been taken in front of the old Slater mansion. Dressed in turn-of-the-century styles were a young woman, a little girl, a man, and a woman holding a baby. The younger woman in the picture had long flowing hair and the familiar, strikingly beautiful face of the woman on the black stallion. Scribbled at the bottom of the photo were the names of the family: Jacob and Martha, Donald, Effie, and Marnie.

Suddenly David felt cold in spite of the sun's bathing warmth. He looked toward the far corner of the room gripping the quilt with icy fingers.

Sleeping on a Victorian sofa, her auburn hair flowing across a velvet pillow, was the same woman.

"Marnie," David whispered.

Chapter 8

David was shivering as he shoved back the quilt and swung his legs over the side of the bed. He carefully pulled himself to a sitting position, but his head swirled while a wave of dizziness and nausea passed through him. He closed his eyes and gripped the bedpost, taking slow, deep breaths until the sickness lessened. He discovered his boots near the bed and stretched his stocking-clad toes into their tops. He carefully dragged them closer and slipped his feet into them, wincing as he reached down to pull them on. He glanced at the sleeping woman and sighed with relief. She lay quiet, her chest rising and falling in peaceful slumber.

David took a deep breath, set his teeth in determination, and forced himself to stand. Sliding his hand along the wall for support, he attempted to take several steps forward, but the room seemed to turn around him spinning faster and faster. Nausea welled up, burning his throat and he fell to the floor with a loud moan.

"Oh no," cried the woman as she awakened and rushed to David's side. "You shouldn't have gotten out of bed. You're in no condition to be up."

David's insides swelled, and he gasped for breath, choking back the putrid flood. The woman grabbed the basin from the table and knelt beside him holding his head while the sickness erupted. Taking a damp cloth from the bedside table, she gently wiped his pallid face.

David looked at her, his eyes wide with panic. He tried to lift his dead weight, but fell back into her arms, shaking and exhausted.

She reached for the quilt and pulled it from the bed to cover him. "I'm sorry," she said easing his head into her lap. "I shouldn't have fallen asleep." She pushed her hair away from her oval face, reaching for the telephone handset she had dropped when she grabbed the basin. "I'd have called emergency air transport or taken you to Slatersville last night, but the storm blew a tree across the highway and knocked out the telephone and power lines." She pushed on the switch. "It's still dead. I've got to get you to a doctor."

The woman's eyes, surrounded by dark lashes, were like sapphire pools on either side of her slim, slightly curved nose. Her tenderness was comforting and clearly showed her anxious concern for David. His gaze was bewildered. She was the same woman in the picture, yet her manner and dress were modern. Dazed and disoriented, David grimaced in pain.

"Ghosts don't go to doctors," he mumbled.

"What? Don't say that. I won't let you die. You're gonna be okay." Her fearful expression changed to one of determination. "I hate to move you, but the highway should be cleared by now. If I help you, can you try to get up?"

David shuddered. "I-I'm so cold."

She tucked the quilt more tightly about him. "I wish I knew more about head injuries. You took an awful blow when your horse struck you."

"Cochise! Where is he?"

"He's in the corral with my horse. He's okay."

"What happened?"

"We startled a cougar in the ravine. He screamed and ran across the trail. The horses were terrified. Your horse reared and his hoof struck you. You fell under us and my horse Chauncy nearly trampled you before I got him under control. I had no idea anyone else was on the trail. It all happened so fast. What were you doing up there?"

"I-I'm an artist. I'd been painting. Wh-who are you?" he asked.

"I'm Kimberly Dawson. What's your name?"

David began shivering more violently. "D-David Young," he struggled to answer through chattering teeth. He closed his eyes with a long quivering sigh.

A worried frown furrowed Kimberly's brow. Hoping to keep

David conscious, she talked as she pulled the pillow onto the floor and slipped it under his head. "Sometimes when the moon is full I go riding at night. I've known that trail since I was a kid. That storm caught me off guard though." Taking two more quilts from the wardrobe, she covered David with them. "It moved in so fast, I was going to hole-up in a nearby cave. Then your accident happened."

David's eyes remained closed.

"David?" she nudged him. "David!" He looked at her, and she forced a smile. "Try to stay with me." She began rubbing his arms and legs under the covers. "I've got to get this chilling stopped. I don't want you to go into shock."

Warmed by the gentle friction of Kimberly's hands and the thick layer of quilts, David's shivering lessened and he became more alert.

Kimberly sighed with relief. "I'm going to get the car ready. Just lie still and rest."

The room felt like it was spinning and so were David's thoughts. The old picture and Victorian furnishings seemed far removed from Kimberly in her sweatshirt and blue jeans. Yet, he sensed that Marnie's immortal image must somehow be closely fused with her very mortal counterpart. Although he had never believed in supernatural apparitions, David's mind was confused by dozens of questions. Could two people, so amazingly alike and still so different, possibly be suspended in time as the same person? Kimberly was human, her touch soft and real. Yet, it was clearly she in the photograph, and three times she had vanished before his eyes. David moaned, too pained and weary to unfold the mystery. His questions slipped beneath the calm forgetfulness of sleep.

Shortly, Kimberly patted David's shoulder. He woke to find her sitting Indian-style on the floor beside him. She smiled. "Hi, feeling a little better?"

"Yeah, I think so," he answered.

"Good. Let's get you to the hospital. Do you think you can stand up?"

"I'll try," David said. "I'm sorry for all the trouble. How did you get me off that mountain last night?"

"Dad always insisted I keep a rope on my saddle so I just used it and Chauncy to lift you onto your horse." She slipped her arm beneath David's back and helped him sit up. I used my blanket and ground cover to keep the rain off you.

David swallowed back nausea, breathing deeply to keep the sickness under control.

"Do you need the basin?"

He swallowed again and shook his head. "How did you get me onto the bed?"

She chuckled. "Your horse is pretty nervous indoors, but I managed to coax him as far as the bedroom door. From there, I just drug you in and pulled you onto the bed."

David looked at her apologetically. "I've put you through a pretty horrendous night, haven't I?"

Her smile was warm and friendly, denying any hardship she had suffered. "Not to worry. Let's get you to the car. See if you can get up," she said, slipping her arms around his chest.

"I'll try," David said. He grasped the edge of the table. With her support he pulled himself upward forcing his legs to take his weight. Shaking under the strain, he swayed and clung to the table. Kimberly slipped his arm over her shoulder and supported him around his waist.

"I'm sorry," he said, trying not to lean on her as he attempted to steady himself.

"Can you make it?" Kimberly asked, wondering how he could walk the distance to the car when he could barely stand.

David took a deep breath, reaching for inner strength. He mustered a slight grin. "Let's go, but I hope you can walk on a merry-go-round. This room sure feels like one."

They struggled through the house and across the deck. Gripping the dash and the roof of the car, David fell into the seat with a groan. Kimberly leaned against the car breathing hard and trembling. "You okay?" he panted.

She nodded, then closed the door and hurried around the car. She pushed the automatic seat control to a reclining position and placed a quilt over him.

"Thanks," David said, catching her wrist and pressing her hand against his chest. "Thanks for everything."

Kimberly smiled. She started the engine and pulled away from her sprawling ranch house. David laid his head against the seat, his mouth drawn in a tight line of pain. "Ghosts don't tremble," he mumbled.

"What?" Kimberly asked, casting him a worried glance, but he didn't answer. She shook her head and patted his knee. "Hang on David. I'll hurry." She drove to the highway and accelerated up the mountain pass toward Indian Summit.

David slept, his pain swallowed by dreams as his mind wandered to his little pond. He knelt on the sandy shore feeling entranced by the strange calmness of the pond and a faint luminous glow on the water. Suddenly, Marnie appeared like a beautiful painting on the eerie surface, reaching her hand toward David. He stood up quickly drawing back, but she touched him. No, it was Kimberly standing beside him who had taken his hand in hers. He felt a comforting peace as she gazed into his face with her reassuring smile. In an instant, David felt himself being pulled from her grasp and her image began to fade. Then she vanished, leaving him alone as ominous clouds crowded around him.

Fear swelled in his chest, and he tried to run from the darkness, but he couldn't move. An icy wind began to blow, ripping him from the ground and sweeping him along with its force. David thrashed about helplessly as it carried him over the pond.

Marnie was standing on the opposite shore, her long hair and white gown whipping about in the fierce gale. She was crying, reaching toward him, as powerful gusts carried David closer and closer toward her.

Chapter 9

"No!" David cried, bolting upright in the seat. Then, he fell backward, grasping his head, moaning and writhing in agony.

"Easy David, we'll be there soon," Kimberly lied. The winding descent to the valley floor, even at a dangerous speed, couldn't possibly take less than forty minutes. Then it was a minimum of ten minutes more to reach Slatersville. "Try to relax," she said in a calm, reassuring voice, but her hand on his chest was shaky.

David groaned softly while the pain gradually decreased. Then he fell asleep. Gripping the steering wheel, Kimberly sped along the winding road.

Suddenly, David rose up. "Pull over," he yelled, pushing the car door open.

Kimberly caught his arm. "David, what's wrong?" she cried slowing to a stop.

"I'm gonna be sick," he moaned. Leaning out the door, his body shook and heaved and his stomach retched violently. Kimberly anxiously watched his fingers turning white as he gripped the door handle. Finally, he lay back in the seat, weak and pale while beads of sweat formed on his brow.

Kimberly wiped his face with a bandanna. "David, are you gonna be okay?" she whispered. "Is there anything I can do for you?"

"Why did you run away at the pond?" he mumbled.

"What? Uh . . ." a red tinge of color crept up Kimberly's neck and spread across her face. "I-I was embarrassed," she stammered, feeling the flush in her cheeks. "I'd just returned from college, and didn't realize Uncle Albert had sold Aunt Effie's place. It's always been my favorite haunt. That morning I saw you painting. I was fascinated, so I watched you. I apologize."

"Where did you go?"

"I . . . uh, climbed a tree," Kimberly answered sheepishly. "You were standing right under it. I was sure you'd look up and find me."

"Climbed a tree," David muttered.

"We'd better get back on the road," she said, hoping to dismiss the incident. "Do you feel well enough to travel?"

"I think so." David smiled weakly, placing his fingers across her hand. "Thanks Kimberly." She nodded and pulled onto the road. David barely whispered, "Ghosts don't climb trees," then his hand fell slowly to his side.

Kimberly glanced at the sleeping man beside her. In spite of his chalky color, David was handsome with strong cheekbones, a straight nose, and a firm jaw and chin framing his slender face. His hair was cropped short on the back of his neck and around his ears and was longer on top and lay damp across his forehead. His eyebrows were light brown, less sun bleached than his hair, and his eyelashes were darker brown. She felt a strange surge of feelings as she smoothed a lock of hair away from his eyes.

Kimberly had been too busy enjoying her parents, her studies, and her horses to get involved with men. Besides, she hadn't met many of them that had her values, or treated a woman with regard. The kindness her father had shown her mother would always stand as a perfect example of the love and respect a sound relationship should be built upon.

Now, deep inside her something whispered that, like her father, this man was different. She felt the same entrancing aura that had drawn her to watch David at the pond surrounding her now with gentle warmth. She had sensed a unique devotion as she'd watched over him through the long preceding night. It was increasing now with powerful force. Her heart felt fluttery as a fondness she had never before experienced swelled inside her. Feeling overwhelming concern for him, Kimberly touched his face with the back of her hand. He was resting peacefully now. His color seemed to be improving, and he was warmer.

Shortly, David awoke, feeling nauseated again. Kimberly pulled to the side of the road. There was nothing in his stomach to throw up, but David's insides retched with a vengeance, while excruciating pressure and pain exploded in his head. Finally, the attack subsided. David collapsed back in the seat, moaning and shivering, his skin cold and clammy.

Kimberly wiped his face and tucked the quilt more tightly about him as tears filled her eyes. A salty drop spilled onto her cheek. "David, I'm so sorry. I wish I could help you."

He looked at her, managing a feeble smile. Reaching up with a shaky finger, he gently brushed the tear away. "I'm okay," he whispered.

Kimberly pulled onto the road, steering the car around the winding curves with desperate determination. David's shivering finally ceased, and he lay so still and pale that she frequently checked to make certain he was breathing.

"Who's the girl in the picture?" David asked.

Kimberly's head whirled toward him. He hadn't moved. *Was he talking in his sleep?* she wondered. "What picture?"

"On your bedside table. She looks like you."

"My great Aunt Marnie," Kimberly answered.

"Marnie Slater?"

Kimberly stared at David, nearly missing a curve. "Yes. How did you know her name was Slater?"

"Had to be related," he mumbled. "Her antique furniture?"

Confused by his question she responded, "Most of it belonged to great Aunt Effie-the other girl in the picture. The baby was my grandfather."

"Who lives in the Slater mansion?"

Kimberly studied David. His eyes were still closed, his skin a chalky pallor. "Uncle Albert, my mom's brother. I don't understand, David. Why all the questions?"

"Ghosts don't cry," he whispered and was quiet again. Kimberly gave a baffled sigh, shaking her head.

The car raced around the last winding curves descending to the valley floor. She accelerated on the level highway, speeding toward town. "Only twenty more miles to go, David," she said.

David didn't respond. Kimberly lightly touched his long, slender fingers speaking softly to herself. "I'll bet he's a good artist. He has graceful hands."

"Thank you," David whispered, wrapping his hand around her small one.

Kimberly was embarrassed, but she didn't pull away. "I-I thought you were asleep," she stammered.

David looked at her flushed face with a faint twinkle in his eyes. "I was," he said. Then still holding her hand, he dozed off again.

He's so cold, and his color isn't good, she thought as they approached Slatersville. *Thank the Lord we're almost there.*

Suddenly David groaned loudly. His body stiffened and his hand tightened on Kimberly's fingers with alarming firmness.

"David, what's wrong? We're only a few miles from the hospital. Please hang on," she pleaded, slamming the accelerator to the floor.

"Call my friend Jerry Stone . . . at the art shop . . ." he groaned. "It's worse, please . . . hurry!" David began shivering violently. "Everything's going numb," he cried. "Can't feel my hands . . . feet . . ." David's grip on Kimberly loosened, and his hand fell limply away. He made a deep sighing moan as his head rolled to the side, and he was silent.

Chapter 10

An empty, helpless feeling struck Kimberly like a blow. She felt panic swelling inside her. "Oh, dear God please . . . not this close to help," she prayed aloud. "Please don't let him die!" She bit her lip, fighting the panic, then began talking to herself. "Hold on and stay in control. Just watch the road and get him there fast."

The scream of a siren came from behind her. Glancing in the mirror, Kimberly saw a patrol car pulling out from a cross-road in hot pursuit. She slowed down enough to let it catch up, and motioned the officer around her. He frowned as he pulled along side, pointing to the edge of the highway.

She lowered the window. "Help me," she called. "There's an injured man in here. I think he may be dying!"

"Follow me," he yelled.

Kimberly looked at David. He was terribly quiet and ashen. She reached for his wrist and felt for a pulse. "Thank you God, he's still alive," she sighed.

The patrolman streaked through town with Kimberly tailing close behind and turned into the emergency entrance of the hospital. He had radioed ahead so several nurses, and a green-clad emergency room doctor were waiting with a stretcher. They wheeled it toward the car, pulling the door open as Kimberly came to a halt.

"What happened?" the doctor asked as they lifted David's limp body onto the cart.

"Head injury," Kimberly exclaimed. "His name is David Young. He was going numb all over just before he lost consciousness. Please help him."

The doctor nodded, checking the pupils of David's eyes as they wheeled him through large double doors.

Suddenly, David began jerking convulsively. "Get Dr.

41

Jonston stat! He's going into a seizure," the doctor ordered as they rushed David into a treatment room and closed the door. Kimberly hovered outside the room pacing the floor.

"Try not to worry," the patrolman said, laying his hand on her shoulder. "He's in good hands. It may be a small hospital, but these guys are the best." He pointed to a row of chairs in the waiting area. "Let's sit down, and you can tell me what happened."

Kimberly obeyed, glancing back at the closed door.

"Is he your boyfriend?" the officer asked.

"No, just a neighbor," she said, but the answer didn't feel right. Then, like a sunrise spreading rays of light, a revelation opened, touching Kimberly's spirit. David wasn't just a neighbor. She sensed a closeness to him that had always been; a kindred bond from somewhere wonderful long ago and far, far away. Somehow, she already knew David, and he was her friend.

A doctor ran down the hall and was quickly directed to David's side. Moments later, a nurse rushed out of the treatment room. She grabbed the phone at the nurse's desk, and her voice blared through the speaker on the wall. "Respiratory therapy to the ER stat! Respiratory therapy to the ER stat!" She replaced the phone, hurried into an emergency supply room, and returned moments later pushing a respirator. A young man in a white coat ran down the hall and held the door wide while the nurse pushed the machine inside the treatment room. He followed her, unwinding the cord to the respirator and pulling a green hose out of a compartment. As the door swung closed, Kimberly caught a glimpse of David surrounded by uniformed figures. His face was an unnatural shade of gray. One of the nurses was depressing an air bag attached to a black mask over David's nose and mouth.

Kimberly's eyes were riveted on the closed door while she informed the policeman of the previous night's events. Although she felt drained and weak, she was relieved to have someone to talk to. It kept her from giving way to the emotional flood that was dammed up inside.

A portable X-ray machine was wheeled into David's room. Nurses bustled in and out, and a laboratory technician hurried to the lab with samples of David's blood. The doctor finally appeared in the hall. His middle-aged face was grave and stony, his jaw set. He approached Kimberly. "Are you a member of Mr. Young's family?" he asked.

"No," she answered. "I was there when . . ."

The doctor cut her off. "He has a serious skull fracture, but swelling and a large blood clot are the life-threatening problems we're facing right now. He needs immediate surgery to remove the clot and bone fragments. Is there any family member we can contact to get permission to operate?"

"I-I don't know," Kimberly stammered. "He did ask me to call a friend. Maybe he knows how to reach David's family."

"Do it quickly please," the doctor ordered, pointing to the phone on the desk. He hurried back to David's side.

Kimberly fumbled through the phone book, locating Jerry's number with trembling fingers.

"Do you want me to call?" the officer asked.

"Yes, please," Kimberly answered, returning to her chair on unsteady feet.

A few moments later, the officer returned. "Mr. Stone is contacting your friend's mother. Then he's coming right over."

Soon, a medium-built man, robust and tanned with curly black hair and dark rimmed glasses burst into the emergency room. He looked anxiously about.

"Are you Jerry Stone?" the patrolman asked.

"Yeah, where's David?" Jerry asked nervously rubbing his hands together.

"The doctors are still working with him." The officer motioned to the closed door. "This is the young lady who brought him in. Will you sit with her while you wait? I need to get back on duty."

"Sure," Jerry said, taking the policeman's seat as he rose to leave. "Hey, I'm really grateful to you for helping Dave," he said, reaching his hand to Kimberly.

"I don't know if I did any of the right things," she answered shaking his hand. "I'm Kimberly Dawson."

"Whoa, girl you're shaking like a leaf. This has been real tough hasn't it?"

She nodded, looking at the closed door. "I-I just hope the doctors can help him." The dam broke and Kimberly began crying.

Jerry slipped his arm around her. "There, honey," he said. "Dave'll make it. He's made of tougher stuff than most people." Jerry held her until her quivering shoulders calmed and she pulled away.

"I'm sorry," she said drying her eyes with the handkerchief Jerry offered. "It's been a frightening ordeal."

"What happened?" Jerry asked. "Can you talk about it?"

Kimberly wiped her nose and nodded, explaining the details of the preceding night and morning. As she described David's final terrifying moments in her car before he lapsed into unconsciousness, Jerry's deep blue eyes grew wide.

"He's that bad?" Jerry stood up, pacing in front of the chairs. Suddenly, his fear erupted into anger. "Why was the idiot riding a horse on a mountain in the middle of the night? What a stupid stunt! If he felt like something bad was going to happen, why didn't he just stay home? He's not thinking with his head anymore." Jerry walked to the treatment room. Staring at the closed door, he slapped his fist into the palm of his hand, then gestured helplessly and returned to his seat.

"You and David must be close friends." Kimberly's voice was sympathetic, trying to calm Jerry's anger.

"Yeah . . . yeah, we are." Jerry sighed and walked back to the closed door. "What's taking them so long?" He paced back and forth, then walked to a window. Bracing himself on his hands, he pressed his lowered head against the glass.

"Can I help you?" Kimberly asked, moving to his side.

"Nah, I'm just worried," Jerry answered, nervously tapping his fingers on the windowsill. "He'll be okay . . . ." Then he clenched his jaw and swallowed hard, slamming his fist against the sill. "He's got to be okay . . ." Jerry stared blankly out the window and took a deep breath. "I don't want to lose him."

Kimberly gazed at the door concealing the intense drama being waged on the other side. "Please God . . ." she whispered.

Finally the door opened, and David was wheeled out on a stretcher. A tube inserted down his throat was attached to a respirator and intravenous solutions were dripping through needles in both arms. He was ghostly white, and the silent shadow of death seemed to hover over him.

Jerry caught his breath in a horrified gasp. He stepped backward, leaning heavily against the wall as his knees went weak. "Oh, God, please help him," he prayed aloud.

Kimberly quickly slid her arm around Jerry's waist.

Shocked and dazed, he put his arm around her shoulder, grateful for her support. Jerry tried to calm himself as he and Kimberly followed David's stretcher to the operating room.

"He isn't breathing on his own, is he?" Kimberly asked the nurse pushing the respirator.

"No," she answered, shaking her surgical capped head. "The machine will keep oxygen flowing to his bloodstream until he can."

As the other blue clad nurses wheeled David's cart through the wide double doors of the surgical unit, Jerry asked, "What are his chances?" His voice sounded choked and husky.

"Try to relax," the nurse answered, pointing to a waiting room. "Dr. Jonston is an excellent neurosurgeon. Your friend will get the best care possible." The doors swung shut behind them with a dull metallic thud.

Jerry and Kimberly stared at the barrier and its "No Admittance" sign. Then Jerry went into the waiting room and sank onto the sofa. He pulled off his glasses and leaned forward, burying his face in his hands.

Kimberly remained in the hall whispering a silent prayer. "Please, Heavenly Father, let him live. I feel something so special. I've just found him. Please don't let me lose him."

"Sometimes David seemed quite rational," Kimberly said as she nibbled on the roast beef sandwich Jerry had insisted she eat. "Other times he wasn't making any sense at all. When he first woke up, he acted frightened, and he made several comments about ghosts."

"Ghosts," Jerry mumbled as an odd expression spread across his face. "Did he mention the legend about Marnie Slater?"

"How did you know he asked about my great Aunt Marnie?"

"Marnie Slater was your great-aunt?"

"Yes," she answered, amazed to hear another stranger mention Marnie's name. "What's going on?"

Feeling a little nervous discussing the subject with a family member, Jerry stammered. "Uh, we talked about the old legend once."

Kimberly's eyes were wide and curious.

Jerry cleared his throat. "It's a strange story. David saw a woman when he was painting. She ran away and he followed, but she disappeared. Ten days ago, the same woman vanished behind the Slater mansion, so I mentioned the legend. David didn't buy the ghost story, but he was pretty confused, and a lot more troubled than he would admit."

"Now I understand," Kimberly said to herself.

"What?" Jerry asked.

"It was me, Jerry. I was the girl who watched him paint."

Jerry's mouth fell open. "You?"

She nodded. "I was at the Slater mansion too. It wasn't nearly being trampled by a horse that frightened him. It was me. That was why he tried to leave while I was sleeping. After hearing that dumb legend, he woke up disoriented from the injury and saw the lighted lantern, my antiques, and me. He must have thought I was Marnie and that I'd somehow taken him back in time."

Jerry moved closer to Kimberly, his eyes narrow and prying. "So tell me then, how did you disappear behind the Slater mansion?"

Chapter 11

Jerry and Kimberly talked for a while. Then exhaustion forced Kimberly's eyes closed and she fell asleep on the couch. When she awoke, Jerry was nervously pacing in the room.

"Have you heard anything?" she asked.

"They're still operating." He gave a worried sigh.

Kimberly looked at her watch. "He's been in there more than five hours." She walked into the hall. "Please, God, guide the doctor's hands with thy love," she whispered, staring at the closed doors.

Jerry watched from the doorway, then stepped behind her squeezing her shoulders. "You really like this guy, don't you?"

She nodded. "I don't understand what I'm feeling. It's hard to explain. I only saw him once until last night, but . . . this is so strange. I feel like I've known him . . . forever." A slight flush touched her cheeks as she smiled and turned to face Jerry.

"I wonder if . . . well, maybe we were kindred spirits before we were born. Is that crazy?"

"I might have thought so a few weeks ago," Jerry said. "I've been doing a lot of thinking though. There's something more to all of this than fate." His gaze shifted to the surgery unit. "A greater hand is at work. For instance was it just chance that you took a weird notion to go riding last night on the same trail? David would have died up there. No . . . somehow you're supposed to be involved. David felt it too. I've never seen him so preoccupied. He lost a lot of sleep thinking about you.

"Hey, I think we could use a break. Let's walk down and get a soda and some chips." Jerry stood up and reached for Kimberly's hand. He folded it in the crook of his arm and escorted her down the hall to the vending machines.

"David's mother must be sick with worry. Is she coming to be with him?" Kimberly asked as they walked.

Jerry shook his head. "I wish she could, but she had a recent laser surgery. It was successful and she's free of pain for the first time in years, but she can't travel for a few months. However, Jan's got more courage than a test pilot. She'd fly her wheelchair here if she could get a fast enough run to get it airborne." He smiled. "Nah, she's cool headed. She'll just sit tight and wait for my call." Jerry pictured David's mother praying with unwavering faith while she waited for news about her only son. He swallowed hard as memories flooded back from his youth. "She's with David," Jerry said almost to himself.

"She's handicapped? What happened? Where's his father?"

Jerry handed Kimberly a soda and motioned her to a chair. Popping open his can, he sat down taking a deep breath. Remembering was painful, but so was waiting and the memories were close to the surface. Jerry shared some of them with Kimberly as his mind opened the doors to the Central High School locker room.

"I hope the new coach will let me assist the team again next year," Jerry said, adjusting David's shoulder pads.

"Nah, I think Sandi Donavan should get the job for our senior year," David said with a mischievous twinkle in his eyes. He pulled his football jersey over his head, grinning as a red tinge of color crept up Jerry's neck. David settled his helmet on his head, and slapped Jerry on the shoulder. "You're a great assistant, but she's prettier than you." He ran outside chuckling to himself, leaving Jerry fuming in the smelly locker room. A moment later, David's helmet appeared in the doorway. "Hey bud, don't let jealousy cost you the best game of the season. You know we can't play a championship game without your loud mouth cheering us on. Let's go!"

Jerry broke into a grin and followed David. When the team thundered onto the field, David pretended not to see the kiss Sandi threw at him as he passed her waving pompoms. Jerry saw it. Although he was grateful for David's response, he could still feel jealous heat smoldering from under his collar. He pulled his jacket higher to cover the red flush. After all, it wasn't David's fault the girls swooned over him. He resembled a Greek god. Jerry himself wasn't bug-ugly though. He had a nice face, and he was every bit as macho as the football jocks, but being shorter was a rotten disadvantage. Jerry had adored Sandi for years, but she didn't even know he was alive.

When the whistle blew for starting time, David walked to the sideline looking for his parents in the bleachers. They always sat on the front row so David could hear them cheering his team to victory. "Jerry, can you see my folks?" he asked, nervously scanning the crowd. "They aren't in their usual spot."

"No, but I'll watch for them. Don't worry . . . they'll be here. They wouldn't miss the game that's sending you to State."

David frowned. "Something's wrong . . . I have a bad feeling."

"They probably just got hung up in traffic," Jerry said, giving David a gentle push toward the team's huddle.

After the huddle broke up, David walked backward to his position on the field, searching the crowd. A patrol car with flashing lights pulled up to the stadium entrance, and David froze in mid-step, his eyes riveted on the policeman as the officer walked toward the home team's sideline.

Watching David's sudden halt, Jerry turned and saw the officer approaching. His eyes swept to the strangers sitting in Doug and Jan's usual place, then back to David. The news the officer relayed was crushing.

The color drained from David's face as the coach motioned Bob Drake to his position on the field. David ran toward the sideline.

Jerry's heart was pounding as he gathered his senses and ran to meet David.

"Jerry, is it my parents?" David asked, his voice cracking.

"Yeah Dave, they've been in a serious accident. The cop said he'd take you to the hospital." David swayed, and Jerry stuck his head under David's shoulder, supporting him off the field.

"How bad?" David whispered.

"They don't know yet. I'll come with you."

"No, Jerry, you'll miss the game."

"I don't care about the game anymore, David. You know that."

In the waiting room, two sixteen-year-old boys sat in stunned silence as emergency personnel rushed about speaking in quiet tones.

Finally, a doctor approached. "I'm Dr. Randall. Your father has extensive internal injuries, and we've got to operate on him. Your mother is still in X-ray. The nurse will take you to the surgical waiting room when we have the results of your mother's CT scan. I'll talk to you later down there."

"Are my parents going to be okay?" David asked.

"We don't know yet. They're both critical right now, but I promise we'll do everything we can for them. I'm sorry I can't give you better news."

"Sir," David stood up, tightly clenching his fists, "the man who hit them . . . the cop said he was drunk." David's eyes were piercing, his mouth drawn in a tight line. "Was he?"

"Yes son. He crossed the centerline, and hit them head on. I'm sorry."

"Where is he now, sir?" David asked, his voice hard and thick.

"He died a few moments ago."

"David sat down, his hands still clenched and a distant expression in his glassy gray eyes. The doctor shook his head as he hurried back to his patient.

Something snapped inside Jerry. "A lousy drunk," he ranted, jumping to his feet, anger hot in the pit of his stomach. "Another stinking lousy drunk! Just take them all out and shoot them so they can't hurt anyone!" He stormed into the hall and kicked a vending machine.

An emergency room volunteer patiently led him across the hall to an empty treatment room. "Let's talk," she said, placing her hand on his shoulder.

He jerked away and sat down, folding his arms defiantly across his chest. "What's to talk about? People like that don't deserve to live. I'm glad he's dead, but why did he have to do this to Doug and Jan first? Why didn't he just take a gun and shoot himself . . . like my old man did?"

Suddenly Jerry was overcome by six years of buried anguish. He leaned forward, drenching the stretcher sheet with his sorrow as he cried fierce wrenching sobs from the depths of his soul.

David opened the door and stood beside Jerry, waiting until Jerry's emotions calmed. Then he touched him with a shaky hand. "Come on Jerry, they want us to go to the other waiting room. Mom's back is broken and . . ." David's body shook as he fought to maintain control. He sucked in a deep breath, "they're taking her to surgery too."

"I'm sorry, Dave." Jerry sniffed, wiping his eyes on his jacket sleeve. "Me crying like a baby isn't helping you."

"No one has a better right, Jerry. Besides, they're your family, too." The boys embraced, strengthening each other.

Several hours later, the doctor placed his hands on both boys' shoulders. "I'm so sorry. Your father died a few minutes ago. His injuries were too severe. They're still operating on your mother. She's going to live, but she'll be paralyzed from the waist down. I wish we could have done more for your father, but your mother will need your strength now."

David stood up, squaring his shoulders. "Thanks for trying so hard." Suddenly, his composure crumbled and he wept in the doctor's arms, his sobs echoing the anguish of his loss. Jerry was dazed with shock. Finally, David sat beside Jerry. They talked about David's parents when their voices could maintain control, numb with disbelief that Doug was gone and Jan would never be the same.

"What am I going to do, Jerry?" David asked. "When your dad died, your sister's husband was due for discharge so Jane and Rich just moved in with you. Mom and I don't have anyone. How am I going to take care of her?"

Jerry shrugged, desperately searching for some ideas. "I don't know, Dave," he moaned. "I really don't know."

David grew silent for a long time. Finally, he rose to his feet as a calm self-assurance came over him. The frightened boy disappeared as a mature young man shouldered the heavy responsibility. "I'll find a way," he said. Walking to the window, he looked up at a million stars. "We'll be okay," he whispered. "With God's help, we'll be okay."

Chapter 12

Kimberly stared at her empty pop can, rolling it in her hand. "What an overwhelming responsibility for a sixteen year old. How did he manage?"

Jerry stood up, offering her his hand as she rose. They walked toward the waiting room. "A life insurance policy paid off their house. They had some health coverage, but the medical bills were still higher than a mountain, so David sold their hardware store to pay the balance. They had Doug's social security and David's wages from two part-time jobs to live on while he finished high school. He applied for college grants and loans, then worked at anything from pumping gas to scrubbing porta-potties while he got his degree in art. I took my minor in art, my major in business, so we formed a partnership. He paints and I sell."

"Success as an artist is hard to achieve, isn't it?"

"Tough as scaling a skyscraper with your teeth, but that never stopped David. He knows how to live a dream. Whenever some big-wig slammed a door in his face, David camped on his window-ledge until the stuffed shirt finally looked at his work."

"Really?" Kimberly's eyes were wide and innocent.

"Well, almost." Jerry chuckled. "David's gutsy enough if he has to be. He was relentless, hounding collectors, galleries, and critics to give him a chance. Of course, if they look, they buy. David's a natural when it comes to art. He's got his foot in the door now. We just got a referral from a gallery that's been showing his work, a big business deal with a lot of high class showings." Jerry stopped and leaned against the door frame of the waiting room. "For the first time since his father's death, David's financially secure." Jerry shook his head, staring at the polished floor. "Until this happened, he finally had a real chance at success. Now . . ."

The surgery doors opened and Dr. Jonston stepped into the hall. The chest and underarms of his scrub suit were drenched in perspiration, and he looked worn and haggard. Kimberly and Jerry exchanged fearful glances.

Dr. Jonston took a deep breath, blowing it out through pursed lips. "Your friend is a determined man," he said as a slight smile creased his face. "Twice I thought I'd lost him, but he hung on with a strength of will I've not often seen. The next twenty-four hours will be critical. He's not breathing on his own and he may remain comatose for some time, but his vital signs are stable. It's too soon to make any predictions at this point, but with his passion for life, he has a good chance of pulling though. We removed the blood clot and bone fragments and repaired the fracture with a metal plate and a skin graft. Swelling will be our greatest concern now, so we'll be watching him closely. He'll be in recovery for a while. You can see him when he's transferred to the Intensive Care Unit."

"Thank you, thank you," Jerry said, gripping the physician's hand in both of his. Unable to say more, he wrapped his arms around Kimberly.

Whispering a silent prayer of thanks, she relaxed in his embrace, releasing her breath in a long sigh.

Jerry kissed her forehead. "God bless you for his chance to live," he said, swallowing the lump in his throat.

Kimberly burst into a smile. "Pulling together for someone really breaks the ice, doesn't it? We were strangers this morning, friends tonight, and now I'm even getting kisses."

Her smile lifted Jerry's spirits. He grinned, reaching for her hand. "Come on, friend. I'll call Jan and then let's go eat. I'm starved."

David appeared extremely fragile against the sterile white sheets of his bed in the Intensive Care Unit. Masses of tubes were connected to his body and four hanging bags dripped fluid and medications into his bloodstream. Cords and wires of a heart monitor attached to his chest transmitted patterns of his heartbeat to a screen above David's bed and to the nurse's station outside his tiny room. The respirator hissed at regular intervals pushing oxygen into David's inert lungs.

Jerry and Kimberly stood beside him as a nurse checked his blood pressure and placed several ice bags against the gauze turban wrapped around his head.

"How is he?" Jerry asked, nervously watching the EKG pattern on the monitor screen.

She smiled and nodded. "He's stable. That's all we can hope for right now. One of you can stay with him if you'd like."

Late that night, Jerry was dozing in the chair in David's room when a nurse hurried in and flipped on the overhead light. An alarm on the monitor was beeping. The heart pattern was rapid and erratic. An instant later, a second nurse arrived.

"He's in trouble. Page the doctor stat!"

Moments later, Dr. Jonston ran to David's bedside and checked the reading on the monitor. He snapped an order to the nurse.

She quickly drew solution from a vile with a syringe, injecting it directly into David's bloodstream through the IV tubing.

Dr. Jonston listened to David's heart. "Don't do this. Come on, buddy, don't stop fighting now. Hang on for a few more hours, that's all we need." He snapped another order to the nurse. The nurse injected another solution into the IV tubing. With concern marring his pleasant features, Dr. Jonston continued listening to David's heart. He darkened the room, peered into David's eyes with an otoscope, and readjusted the drip on both IV infusion pumps. Then he listened again to his patient's heartbeat.

Finally, he nodded at Jerry. "Swelling is affecting the brain function that controls his heart and lungs. He was threatening cardiac failure, but we stabilized him with heart stimulants. We'll be monitoring him very closely. He's holding on."

Jerry had stood against the wall with clenched fists and a rigid jaw, watching his friend wavering on the brink between life and death. As the doctor returned to the nurse's station, Jerry dropped into the chair, crying quietly with his head in his hands.

Kimberly slipped to his side and touched his shoulder. "Jerry, the nurse told me what happened. You get some rest. I'll sit with him for awhile."

Jerry nodded, wiping his eyes as he quickly left the room.

Kimberly moved to David's bedside, took his cold limp hand in hers, and pressed it to her lips. Surveying the tubes and wires supporting his life and watching the artificial rise and fall of his chest, she felt overwhelmed at the odds of the battle he was waging. She allowed herself a brief moment of despair. Then, reaching deep inside herself for greater faith, she spoke to him as if he were conscious. "David, Jerry told me that you aren't a quitter. This must be the hardest thing you've ever done. Draw on your courage now. You mustn't give up. Please fight your way back." Tenderly rubbing his arm, she whispered, "Stay with us. We love you . . . I-I love you."

She lingered at his side, caressing his hand and wondering if somehow, her life, her strength, might help him cling to the weak spark of life that still burned within his soul. "Please dear Lord, make him stronger," she prayed. "Please don't let him slip away."

Several hours passed. The ICU staff tried to get Kimberly to sit down, but she remained standing at David's side. *If I can just hold onto him until morning, maybe he can hold on, too,* she thought.

Finally, a nurse pulled the chair over to the bed. "Honey, you've been standing here too long. You've got to rest. We don't usually allow anything to block our access to the patient. Just move the chair quickly if he has any problems."

Kimberly nodded and sat down. She watched the steady pattern on the monitor and listened to the soft beep each time the respirator filled David's lungs. Then she fell asleep, her head resting beside David's hand, which was still firmly clasped in her own.

Chapter 13

The rays of the morning sun peeped through a window and spread bright sunbeams across the wall. They reached the bed, falling upon Kimberly's soft waves of hair and danced on her face. She moaned and turned away from the light, blinking at her surroundings. Suddenly, she remembered where she was.

"David," she said, sitting upright. She was still holding his hand and it was warm. He lay motionless, but his face seemed less swollen; the grayness was gone. She gently pressed her fingers against his cheek. It felt warm, too. "Thank you Heavenly Father. We got our miracle." Settling back in the chair, she sighed as anxiety melted into the comfort of hope. "Thank you for keeping him through the night," she said softly.

A few moments later, a nurse came in to work with David. Kimberly got an update on his condition, then went to the waiting room outside the ICU. Jerry was sleeping on the couch.

She tiptoed out and closed the door, then drove to the Slater mansion to freshen up, borrowing a change of clothes from her cousin.

Returning to the hospital, she purchased breakfast at the cafeteria, then sat at a patio table outside watching two sparrows scraping over a bread crust. "Share it," she mumbled, swallowing a bite of scrambled egg. "Life's too precious. Don't waste it fighting." The birds didn't listen. Kimberly broke her toast into pieces and tossed them toward the birds. She smiled as several more sparrows fluttered to the ground, pecking and scraping over the toast. "You should have been raised by my Dad," she said, remembering occasional squabbles she'd had with her cousins.

Her father had been a kind man, who believed everything he had was a gift from God and should be shared. She'd learned through his example and gentle persuasion that her favorite toy was still hers when her cousins and friends were through playing with it. She chuckled to herself. The only thing he'd ever been selfish with was his secret fishing hole.

Growing up on a horse ranch with her father as her mentor had been a choice experience for Kimberly. She had earned her business and specialized degrees in range and livestock management. She was finally ready to rebuild the herd and carry on the work she had inherited and loved. Yet all the knowledge gained in four years of college seemed of far less importance than the values and lifetime of wisdom she had learned from her father. *I wish I could talk to him now*, she thought.

It had been thirty-six hours since the scream of a cougar had set in motion David and Kimberly's fateful meeting on the rugged slopes of Thunder Mountain. That fearful night seemed long ago, more like a dream. Yet her world had been permanently altered, touched by a presence yet intangible, as David lay in silent battle. What part would this handsome stranger play in her life? Although she had only premonitions to base her feelings on, Kimberly was certain of one truth. She couldn't imagine any future without him in it.

She shook her head. *Oh Dad, I wish you were here. I need your advice.* Kimberly set her napkin down with a sigh. *I could call Mom. She's such a treasure, but she's too sensible. She'd tell me to come back to earth and let time decide the future. She's wise, but Dad was wiser. He knew better how to listen to the inner promptings. Oh well, sometimes you just have to be crazy and follow the path that doesn't make sense.*

Kimberly rose, brushing her crumbs onto the patio. "You might as well fight over these, too," she said smiling at the chirping and flutter of wings behind her as she entered the cafeteria. She bought another tray of food and returned to the waiting room.

"Jerry," she said, gently shaking him awake. "I'm sorry to disturb you, but your eggs will get cold."

Jerry sat up and ran his hand across the black shadow of stubble on his chin. "Thanks," he said, putting on his glasses.

He looked at Kimberly with anxious eyes. "How's David?"

Kimberly smiled. "The nurse said there's no change, but he looks better. His color has improved, and he's warmer. I have a good feeling about him."

"I hope you're right," Jerry said, smoothing his tangled hair. "He really scared me last night. For a few minutes . . . I thought it was all over." Jerry shuddered.

"How did you and David become so close?" Kimberly asked, handing Jerry his tray. "Your friendship seems quite unique."

"We lived next door to each other," Jerry answered. A twinkle crept into his sad eyes. "I had older sisters, but David and I both wanted a brother. When we were nine, we summoned the courage of warriors, poked our fingers with his Cub Scout knife, and mingled our blood, vowing to be brothers forever. It wasn't just a kid thing with us. We really meant it." Jerry took a sip of juice. "Didn't matter whether we were being good or getting into trouble, we were always in it together. Our mothers teamed up and kept us from wrecking the neighborhood, until my mom died of leukemia when I was ten." Jerry grew quiet.

Kimberly glanced away. "That must have been awfully hard."

Jerry quickly locked the memory away. "Well, that was a long time ago." He took a deep breath and continued. "Dave and I were always up to something. When we were in first grade, David's folks bought a box of oranges for Christmas. David and I liked to throw rocks at the graffiti on an old warehouse across our alley. Those oranges were great ammunition for target practice. We thought we were only taking a few at a time but the box got empty really fast. Jan stood over us, hands on her hips, a pancake turner in her hand, and blood in her eyes, demanding to know what happened to her oranges. We told her we had eaten some, but we were sure we hadn't eaten that many. She never said another word, but I could have sworn I saw smoke rising from her ears. A few minutes later, we heard her on the phone, asking my mom if I'd been spending a lot of time in the bathroom." He chuckled at the memory.

"We thought we were in the clear until David's dad took out the trash and saw the smashed oranges in the bottom of the dumpster. Then he noticed the side of the warehouse. All we could do the next week was make faces at each other through our bedroom windows."

Jerry found comfort in reminiscing. He let himself drift back to by-gone days with David, and Sandi Donavan, and Mary Jo Lonkey. Mary Jo had been Jerry's worst nightmare, but now he remembered her with a certain fond amusement. Her role was vital to their story.

"You stupid, slimy sack of fish guts!" Jerry yelled, kicking at Mary Jo. "You're dog meat!" At the other end of the sixth-grade hall, David whirled around as Mary Jo jumped back and Jerry's foot sent the books under her arm plummeting across the floor.

"Jerry Stone!" Mrs. Deacon's voice froze Jerry in place while her squat bulky frame waddled up to him. Her pudgy fingers gripped the top of his ear as she pulled him toward the principal's office.

David followed at a safe distance and waited outside in the hall until Jerry came out, his head hanging low. "What the heck got into you?" David asked.

"I hate her," Jerry snarled. "Mary Jo is always getting me into trouble, even if I don't do anything. I'm in Mr. Zachary's office more often than he is."

"What happened today?"

"She pushed me too far this time. Somehow, she overheard me telling you I liked Sandi Donavan. When you were sick yesterday, Mrs. Deacon took me to the office during last period to re-take that dumb history test. Mary Jo blabbed everything I told you to the whole class. Then, she said I told her I kissed Sandi behind the school dumpster. When Sandi came to school this morning, she hit me. Stan Corbet told me why. I swear Mary Jo's gonna be dead tonight."

"Cool down Jerry. Do you want to spend the whole year in Zachary's office? You have to use your brains not your temper to get even with a witch like Mary Jo. Come over tonight, and we'll make a plan for revenge that will be better than murder. By the time we finish with her, she'll wish she was dead."

That night, shining flashlights in the dark corners of David's basement, the boys found the treasure they were looking for. Jerry carefully wrapped it in a napkin and stuck it in his pocket.

The next morning, David stood watch while Jerry deposited the napkin in Mary Jo's lunch box. They could hardly contain themselves, but imagining the consequence of getting caught kept them under control. When the class finally swarmed into the lunchroom, David and Jerry sat in the far end of the room and innocently waited.

The suspense was short. A piercing shriek soon rose above the noisy chatter of the students. Except for Mary Jo's wailing a sudden hush filled the lunchroom. Several teachers hurried to her rescue, removing the dead mouse that had rolled from the napkin onto her bologna sandwich.

Throughout the following week, Mary Jo was plagued by dead spiders and bugs in her desk and books. One day, Jerry and David thought she was going to faint when she reached into her school supply box and pulled out an earthworm, sun dried and stiff as a pencil.

One evening, David and Jerry went to the canal to fish. As usual, Jerry reeled in several nice trout while David's limp line only grew taut once when it snagged under the bridge. David climbed down to untangle it and started to laugh. "We've got a new weapon, Jerry. I just snagged a big frog."

The next morning, Jerry and David sat winking at each other as the class gathered in the schoolroom, milling about and sharpening their pencils.

A strange echoing sound like a burp came from Mary Jo's desk. Everyone looked at her. With wide, innocent eyes, she put her hand to her mouth, shaking her head.

"How rude, Lonkey." Gary Jakes laughed, pointing at her.

"What did you eat last night?"

David and Jerry suppressed their snickers, feeling like their insides would burst as Mary Jo glared at Gary, red-faced and angry. Tossing her blond curls, she stuck her nose in the air and opened her desk lid. A loud croak filled the air, and the frog leaped into her lap.

A blood-curdling scream ripped through the halls of the school. Mrs. Deacon and several other teachers rushed to the classroom. Mary Jo was standing on top of her desk stomping her feet and screeching in horror. The entire class stood gaping in shock as the frightened frog hopped under a shelf of science books. Jerry and David had forgotten to lay low and keep cool. They were hysterical, laughing and holding their bellies while tears streamed down their faces.

"Those were great days." Jerry chuckled, still enjoying the story after sixteen years. "We didn't even mind spending the whole day in the principal's office writing, "I will not tease Mary Jo Lonkey." Jerry finished his juice, rolling the last few drops around in the bottom of his glass. "David and I never had much money, but we didn't care. We could always find something exciting to do."

Jerry's smile faded as his mind returned to the Intensive Care Unit. He set his tray down, then stood and looked out the door at David's room. Blinking hard, he mumbled, "Man, life would be empty without him."

Chapter 14

The tall stately frame of a man clothed in white stood against a brilliant background of clouds. His eyes were clear and penetrating, yet soft with warmth, and a smile creased his face. David recognized his father. A feeling of overwhelming joy surged through him. His soul ached to embrace his father, to be wrapped again in the loving comfort of his arms. David reached for him, but was unable to move toward him. Somewhere in the darkness behind him a soft touch held David, gently pulling against the bright light that surrounded his father.

Life is a strange companion, Kimberly thought as she stood beside David holding his hand. *One can never be prepared for the unpredictable corkscrews it flings at us from every angle, or for the passions, joys, and agonies its instability brings to bear. Everything that has been is swept away like a dream, and life is new, strange, and uncertain.* She gently caressed David's fingertips. *You and me, strangers, yet somehow friends from the beginning of time. Where will life and its mysteries take us? This waiting and wondering is unbearable, yet it's all that can be done.*

She gazed out the window at two sparrows tugging on a worm. "Are you still fighting?" she said to herself. "Don't you know there's always another worm just under the surface?"

A raspy sound came from the tube in David's mouth. Kimberly gasped as his chest heaved between the regular pushes of the respirator. With hope swelling inside her, she rushed to get a nurse.

The nurse entered the room as David's chest heaved a second time. "This is good, David," she said, switching the respirator from the control mode to assist control. "Come on, give it another try." David's chest surged again and the machine responded with a push of oxygen.

"What's happening?" Kimberly asked breathlessly.

The nurse smiled, a look of triumph in her eyes as another heave of his chest was followed by the respirator's hiss. "He's triggering the machine. He's starting to breathe on his own."

Jerry shaved the stubble from his face and stepped into the shower. He welcomed the warm water as it sprayed over him, relieving the tautness in his muscles. He dressed, called Jan with an update on David's condition, and then drove back to the hospital.

Kimberly met him in the hallway outside the ICU. A misty haze in her eyes formed multiple Jerrys. She smiled at them all. "He's trying to breathe," she said.

"Yes!" Jerry shouted, smacking his fist into the palm of his hand. He grabbed Kimberly in his arms and whirled her around. Then he just held her close and glanced heavenward. "Thank you, God," he whispered.

Throughout the afternoon, Kimberly or Jerry sat with David, feeling encouraged as the flow of the respirator became more and more regular. That evening Kimberly was exhausted. She needed to check on the horses anyway, so she followed Jerry's urging to go home to rest. She stood by David's bedside for some time, watching his steady breathing, then softly touched his cheek and left the room.

Jerry slept in the chair, awakening often to listen for the steady hiss of the respirator.

The next morning, Dr. Jonston watched his patient. "Let's switch the respirator to intermittent mandatory control," he told the nurse. "I think he's ready to try on his own. Monitor his oxygen level for two hours, then order blood gases drawn and call me with the results."

Jerry anxiously watched from the corner as the therapist readjusted the respirator. It stopped hissing and all was silent. David's chest jerked and quivered, heaved several more times, then expanded as he sucked life-giving breath deep into his lungs. Jerry relaxed his grip on the chair arms leaning back with a deep sigh.

The doctor listened to David's breathing as it became deeper and more regular and nodded with satisfaction. As he left the room, he smiled at Jerry. "Your friend is a determined scrapper," he said. "The odds could have beaten him a number of times, but I think he's in the clear now. We won't know the full extent of possible brain damage until he's conscious, but it's safe to assume he will live."

"Thanks for everything," Jerry said. "We owe you his life." He hurried to call Kimberly and David's mother with the good news.

Jerry returned to David's bedside and stood watching him. Although David's breathing was strong and steady, Jerry's relief was overshadowed by David's still silent form. "I don't know what the future holds my friend," he said, placing his hand on David's shoulder. "Whatever happens, we'll pull through it together, like we always have." He moved to the chair and sat down as visions from long ago filled the hospital room. In spite of painful memories, the past was more comforting right now, the present still too uncertain.

"Hey Jerry, Dad got someone to cover the store so we're going camping Wednesday after we close. Mom and Dad want you to come. It won't be fancy, hot dogs and trout again, but you know Mom makes a killer potato salad. Think you can talk your dad into it?"

"Who knows . . . depends on which mood he's in when we start loading my stuff into your truck."

Wednesday afternoon, as the truck wound through the sagebrush covered hills toward Hansen Reservoir, David spoke above the rush of the wind. "Man, I'm glad your dad gave in." He rested his elbows and hands on the rim of the pickup bed and stretched his lanky legs over the cooler. "I wonder what my dad said to make him change his mind."

"I don't know, but I'm sure glad Doug is on my dad's good side. Dad hates to be left alone. He wants me where he can yell at me to fix him a sandwich or bring him a beer so he doesn't have to get up from the TV. Your father is the only reason I get to go anywhere. Dad says 'yes' to Doug, when he'd yell anyone else out of the house. There's no way he would have accepted any other offer to pay the rest of my scout camp fees the last three years. It really chapped me when Doug had to help me this year, though." Jerry shook his fist at the air. "I'd saved enough from mowing lawns to pay my way. Then my old man took fifty dollars out of my savings account one week before I had to turn it in.

"He's always borrowing my money. Thinks he's paying me back by giving me a five-dollar bill whenever it suits him. Now, I stash my earnings in a sock drawer so he can't spend my money on his beer." Jerry angrily punched his sleeping bag with each emphasized word.

"Hey no problem, Dad understands. Besides, you're like his kid anyway."

"I know," Jerry sighed. Then he sat up and smiled. "It was a blast, white-water rafting, getting soaked all day, then shivering around the fire at night. If it weren't for scouting and your family, I wouldn't even have a life." A look of sadness marred his fourteen-year-old face. "I don't know Dave. Since Mom died, he just gets weirder every year. I hardly even remember the good times anymore. My sisters can't stand him. Jane married that ditsy soldier and ran off to California. Stephanie got her scholarship halfway across America just to get away, and Sally practically lives at her friend Marsha's house so he can't yell at her." Jerry shook his head and leaned back against the folded tent in the rattling bed of the pickup. "Can you imagine how terrific hot dogs, gutting fish, slapping mosquitoes, and not getting in trouble for three whole days sounds?" Jerry yawned, his curly black head bouncing against the tent canvas. Eventually he fell asleep, resting better than he had for days.

The old green pickup followed the winding road back into corridors of Jerry's mind, back to the halls of Central High School.

At the top of the staircase, Jerry whirled to face David. "You rotten jerk!" he yelled, doubling his fists in David's stunned face. "Since sixth grade I've been spilling my guts to you about Sandi. Now I find out my so-called best friend asked her to go to the Junior Prom. While you're dancing with my girl, I'll be home washing baby bottles and changing dirty diapers."

"Jerry, she's not your girl," David spouted, feeling a little hot under the collar. "She's not wearing your ring. Besides, I never asked her out until you told me you didn't want to go to Prom. For Pete's sake, I don't know what you're so riled about! It's only a dance. I didn't ask her to marry me. She hasn't even accepted yet. Why the heck did you tell me you weren't going if you wanted to ask her?"

Jerry turned his back. Leaning on the upstairs railing, he hung his head. "I told you I wasn't going because she turned me down. She'll always turn me down. Just once, I'd like to be as good as . . . I'm sorry Dave. It's not your fault."

Without looking back, Jerry walked down the stairs bearing the hurt of a thousand heartaches.

That evening, Jerry's doorbell rang. He waded through toys to answer it, tripping over a teddy bear.

"Hey, Jerry. Still baby-sitting?" David asked.

"Yeah, Jane and Rich don't get off until nine all week."

"I've got someone lined up to take care of Mom Friday night. What do you say we find Jane a sitter and take in a movie? Then we can sack out in your garage and play Monopoly 'til dawn."

"But that's Prom night, Dave," Jerry stammered.

"Sandi dumped me too. Left me hanging until four days before Prom, then discarded me for Gary Jakes. She'd heard he didn't have a date yet, so she was holding me in reserve in case he asked someone else."

"Hey, man, I'm sorry."

"Don't be. I was going to cancel anyway after I found out she'd refused you. I just wish I'd had the pleasure of dumping her first." David picked up the teddy bear and punched its belly. "What a wench. I know you're crazy about her Jerry, but she doesn't deserve you."

"Dave, there are a hundred other girls who'd pawn their glass slipper for a one-hour invitation to the Prom with you. You should ask someone else."

David bopped Jerry on the head with the bear. "Eh. What's a Junior Prom anyway?" He said with a grin.

In the tiny room of the intensive care unit, Jerry's memories of David, loyal, full of life, fun loving, and bursting with energy, seemed very threatened. He looked at his friend's unconscious form with an enormous emptiness in the pit of his stomach.

He remembered the long agony waiting in another hospital beside his grieving friend. Now Jerry waited alone. Dr. Jonston had mentioned possible brain damage, and David had gone numb just before he slipped into a coma. What if his mind had been damaged? What if he was paralyzed? What if he couldn't ever paint again? What if the David, Jerry had always known, no longer existed?

Jerry pushed the bleak thought away. He stood up and walked to the window. Suddenly, a moan escaped David's lips. Jerry rushed to his side.

David stirred, moving his head, then moaned again. Instantly a nurse was beside him. Jerry held his breath as David pulled his knees up, rolling from side to side.

"Easy David," the nurse said. "You're doing fine. Just take it easy."

David groaned and winced, his face grimacing with pain as his hands slowly raised; he reached toward his head.

"He's not paralyzed," Jerry cried, gripping the bed rail. "Dave, I'm here," he said. David's eyelids fluttered then opened, and he stared blankly toward the ceiling. A look of dismay spread across Jerry's face. "Oh no, is he blind?" he whispered.

The nurse shook her head. "I don't know. Sometimes it just takes a while for them to come around."

"Oh please God, don't let him be blind." Jerry took David's left hand in his. "Dave, can you see?" he asked. "Dave, it's me, Jerry. Can you hear me?' For a dark second, Jerry feared deafness too. David lay motionless his eyes fixed on nothing.

Finally, David blinked several times and slowly turned his head toward Jerry. His eyes moved erratically for a few moments, then they seemed to focus as they rested on Jerry's drawn face. A flicker of recognition eased David's confused expression. He sensed Jerry's grip and weakly pressed his fingers against the hand that held his so tightly.

Jerry's clenched jaw relaxed as his face widened in a grin. He gripped David's shoulder with his other hand. "Welcome back, Dave," he said trying to control the huskiness of his voice. "Man, did you have me worried!"

Dr. Jonston hurried into the room. "Your doc's here. I'll be back in a few," Jerry said. He pulled his hand away with a quick squeeze as he left the room.

Jerry flopped onto the waiting-room couch. Removing his glasses, he rubbed his eyes. The fear of loss had been so intense during the past three days that even the relief he felt now couldn't dispel its lingering shadow. Inside he wanted to cheer. Outside he just felt dead-dog-tired. Finally, he got up and called Jan and Kimberly.

Chapter 15

David's father stood surrounded by light, his beloved face and presence comforting his son. David wanted to run to him, to throw his arms around him, but he couldn't move. Then he felt himself being drawn backward into a dark corridor. Still reaching out to his father, David drifted further from the light. His father smiled and waved then was hidden to David's view.

Lost in blackness, David became aware of intense, throbbing pain swelling in his head as though it would burst. A familiar voice resounding above muffled noises like an echo called him out of the shadows. Struggling against weakness, David opened his eyes, but he couldn't move them. The words were pleading, and David felt a strong desire to obey. Forcing his eyes to search for the voice, he saw a blurry form above him. Finally his vision cleared, and he looked into Jerry's concerned face. Feeling confused, uncertain where he was or why, David was relieved to see his friend. He felt Jerry's fingers pressing on the palm of his left hand. He sensed his friend's anxiety and made a feeble attempt to reassure him by squeezing his hand.

Jerry grinned, and his words were clear this time. "Welcome back, Dave. Man, did you have me worried."

The next few days were a painful haze. Jerry was frequently at his bedside or in the chair in his room. David was encouraged by his company and responded to Jerry's questions, but nothing seemed clear. He was aware of the doctor and nurses touching him, testing his reflexes or taking vital signs, but he was oblivious to hours, days, or nights.

Somewhere in the cloudy cognizance was another face. A beautiful woman, with auburn waves of hair often lingered at his bedside. She called him by name, her smile and touch were warm and tender. He felt a gentle stirring when she was with him. He recognized her, but she seemed mixed up with his dreams.

Gradually his mind became more alert. However, he still slept most of the time and often asked the same questions over and over, unable to retain the answers.

Then one morning, David woke up feeling less pressure and pain, and the foggy sensation in his head had cleared. "Is this all you ever feed a man around here?" he asked the nurse as she placed a thermometer in his mouth.

"Oh, we're hungry today, are we? I'll call the doctor and get you some lunch." The thermometer beeped and she removed it.

"I don't need a doctor," David said. "Just feed me. I'm famished!"

She smiled and left the room. A short time later, she returned carrying a tray.

"What's this?" he protested. "I'm starving to death, and you bring me Jell-O and broth?"

"Sorry," she said, raising the head of his bed upright. "Doctor wants to see if you can tolerate liquids today. If you can keep it down, he'll put you on a regular diet tomorrow."

"I could be dead by then." David's hand felt numb and awkward as he picked up the spoon. It slipped from his fingers and clattered onto the tray. His arm dropped limply to his side. "My hand won't work!" he cried in alarm.

"You have some right-side weakness David, but it shouldn't be permanent. You'll start physical therapy as soon as the doctor feels you're ready." The nurse gave him an encouraging smile. "Try eating with your left hand until you get your strength back."

"You might as well ask me to feed myself with my foot," he grumbled as she left the room. Worry shadowed David's face as he clumsily shoveled a spoonful of gelatin into his mouth.

Jerry closed his gallery for lunch and drove to the hospital. When he walked into David's room he halted in surprise, and then burst into a broad grin. "Hey Dave, you look good vertical. How are you feeling?"

"Hungry," David growled. "And they won't feed me."

Jerry moved to the bedside table and examined the partially-eaten food. "Yuck, how do they expect you to get well on this junk?"

"I just have to get it down. If I don't throw up, they said I can have real food tomorrow."

"This would make me throw up," Jerry quipped.

"Shut up! You're not helping," David complained. "Man, I feel like I've been trapped in a fog." He took another spoonful and swallowed the cool gelatin. "How long have I been spaced out?"

"About a week," Jerry answered. He lowered his eyes. "You nearly left us for good several times."

"I feel like it," David said, touching his bandage. "I only remember one heck of a pain in the brain. Everything else is scrambled together. Who's the woman that comes in? I know her from somewhere in all this jumble, but I don't even remember her name."

As Jerry reviewed the occurrences of the past few weeks, David closed his eyes. Reaching inside his mind, he began to sort out his confused memories. When Jerry finished, David remained quiet as his thoughts gradually became clear. Then he spoke. "She was the girl at the pond."

"Yeah, that was Kimberly. I thought you'd gone to sleep again. You've done that a lot this week. You'd be talking and just drift off in the middle of a sentence."

"I was just remembering," David said. "She climbed a tree."

"What?"

"That's how she disappeared. She climbed a tree."

"What a bluff." Jerry laughed. "You won't believe how she vanished behind the old mansion, either."

"You know? How?" David asked.

"Your ghost went through the fence," Jerry whispered with a mysterious grin. "She had to water her uncle's garden while he was on vacation. In her hurry to make an appointment, she forgot the gate key. So she pulled off a loose board that she and her cousins used to sneak through to go to the candy store. You must have gotten there just as she put it back in place."

"I had nightmares about a loose board . . ." David muttered, shaking his head. "Tell me what you know about her, Jerry."

"Kimberly lives across the valley from you. Her place and yours were part of a homestead belonging to Effie Slater. Marnie and Effie are Kimberly's great-aunts. Effie sold the Dawson's all her land except your place when Kimberly was born.

"Kimberly's father died two years ago. Her mother sold their livestock and leased out the ranch. Then she married an oil man from Texas, and Kimberly inherited the estate. Kimberly just graduated from college and returned home, planning to rebuild a horse-ranching business."

"That's why I'd never seen her before." David leaned back against the pillow and sighed. "Man, I'm beat." He pushed his tray away. "Lay me down a little Jerry. I've got to rest for a while . . . sorry."

Lowering David's head, Jerry smiled. "Don't worry about me. I'll just bore myself with a magazine."

"Thanks for being here for me." David mumbled as he closed his eyes. "Thanks . . . for always being . . . there . . ."

Jerry stood beside his sleeping friend. *How could I do less? You've always been there for me*, he thought, recalling years of loneliness after his mother's death and the agony of growing up with an alcoholic father.

Jerry sat down in the chair and watched brightly colored roses bobbing in the breeze outside David's window. He couldn't stop the memories. They swirled into the room like a churning flood, engulfing Jerry in their murky depths.

Chapter 16

Ten-year-old Jerry carried a bouquet of roses, withering and brown-tipped from the frost, to his mother's bedside. "Mom, Jan said I could pick some of her flowers. I know they're not very pretty anymore, but I hope they make you feel better."

His mother took them in her frail hand. Deeply breathing their sweet fragrance, she smiled. "Come here, Son." She hugged him, running her fingers through his hair. "Thank you Jerry, roses are always beautiful. I love you. You're such a good boy." Wearily she closed her eyes and went to sleep. She never awakened, slipping away during the night.

The next morning, Jan, Doug, and David brought a freshly baked loaf of bread to the Stones and offered their condolences. Jan helped the girls clean the house, preparing for guests who would be paying their respects. Doug drove Jerry's father, Robert Stone, to the mortuary to make funeral arrangements.

Jerry lay on his bed trying to hide his grief under the pillow he'd pulled over his head. David sat beside him, drying his own tears on his shirtsleeve.

Jerry spent many hours at David's house during the next few weeks. Often he appeared on the doorstep looking like a little lost soul. Jan would gather him in her arms, rocking and comforting him. The boys played like old times, the terrible emptiness forgotten until Jerry had to return home, where his mother's vacant chair was a cold reminder of his loss.

In time, the emptiness seemed more normal, but other things were different. Jerry's father had grown somber and moody, spending his time either sitting for hours in front of the television or sleeping. He went to work regularly, but returned grumpy and hostile. When he started drinking, life became more difficult for Jerry and his sisters. The next five years were troubled and stormy, controlled by Robert's dramatic mood swings between depression and anger. Sometimes he didn't speak to anyone for days. Then he'd suddenly fly into a rage, swearing and throwing things around. He yelled at his children without provocation, his words harsh and cutting.

At Doug and Jan's insistence, Jerry or his sisters called them when Robert went into a tirade. Instantly, the Youngs appeared on the doorstep requesting the children's help with some dreamed-up project or task. Robert never refused. He found his behavior and lack of control frightening, but he was too sick and addicted to believe he could be helped.

At the Young's, simple tasks were followed by a delicious meal and fun or games while Robert's temper cooled. There were always encouraging words and hugs to ease the pain. How Jerry loved these good people!

David was quick to defend Jerry from cruel taunts the neighborhood kids had picked up from gossip. Jan repaired ripped shirts and treated bruised lips or blackened eyes. If David came home in tatters, she'd send for Jerry, knowing he would need attention, too.

David helped Jerry with his chores, trying to keep him out of trouble, but sooner or later some spark of irritation would set Robert off. Refusing to leave his friend to bear it alone, David also endured the drunken ravings that were heaped on Jerry's shoulders. By the time Jerry was fifteen, Robert had become more threatening and had started occasionally slapping Jerry around.

Several times, Doug Young delayed taking action against Robert only because Jerry begged him not to. Finally, Doug could tolerate no more. He demanded that Robert seek help or a report of child abuse would be filed against him. Robert agreed and entered a rehabilitation center.

Jerry stayed with David for the next month. He brightened, improving in school, and becoming more carefree.

Too soon, the day of Robert's release came. Jerry tried to be optimistic, but he couldn't fight off a feeling of dread. "Pray for us, David," he said as he left David's house and returned home to greet his father.

Several weeks passed, and Jerry began to feel more at ease. He even saw occasional glimpses of the pleasant man his father used to be as they shared a football game on TV or played checkers. Then one day, he came home from school, and his heart plummeted into the blackness of despair. His father should have been at work, but the car was parked in the driveway.

"Something is wrong," Jerry told David as a shadow of fear passed across his face. "I can feel it."

"Want me to come with you?" David asked.

Jerry shook his head. "I'll call you," he said dryly. He slumped his shoulders, dragging his feet toward the house. He knew what he would find and he didn't want to face David with his shame. Opening the door, he leaned against the frame with a groan. Several empty six-packs lay strung around the living room and the house was in disarray. Jerry gathered the empty bottles. He stooped to clean a bag of spilled chips from the floor and saw a picture lying beside the chair. It was his mother, smiling and beautiful in her wedding gown.

He picked it up, gently brushing away some crumbs and turned around. Suddenly he froze. His father was watching him from the hall. A dark mood surrounded the man as he staggered forward, leaning on the back of a chair.

"I didn't make it, Son. I can't quit. I'm sorry . . . I really wanted to, but I just can't."

All the frustrations of the past five years raged inside Jerry, while hope crumbled like clay at his feet. "You don't want to, or you would!" he yelled. "We all lost Mom. Don't you think we hurt too? How could you do this to me? I just started believing in you again." He shook his mother's picture at Robert. "I'm glad she's not here because what you're doing would kill her." Jerry glared at his father and the coldness of steel filled his heart. "You're nothing but a coward. I hate you!" he yelled. "I hate you!"

Robert threw himself at his son. "You can't talk to me like that," he roared, letting his fist fly into Jerry's face.

David had hesitated outside, watching Jerry's defeat as he

went inside. He lingered nearby, aching for his friend, but respecting his right to face his burden in privacy. David stiffened when he heard Jerry's angry voice, then sprang into action at the threatening tone of Robert Stone's words. He burst into the house just as Robert's blow hurled Jerry against the table, shattering the lamp. Shards of glass fell around Jerry as he crumpled to the floor.

Robert lunged at Jerry again, but David jumped in front of him, his fists clenched and fire in his eyes. "Leave him alone, Bob," he yelled. A clumsy blow from the back of Robert's hand connected with David's stomach, pushing him aside. David doubled over, grasping Robert's arm to halt his angry advance toward Jerry. "I said, leave him alone," he gasped, trying to catch his breath. Robert shoved David backward. David fell over a magazine rack, watching helplessly while Robert rushed at his son.

Doug Young had just pulled into his driveway when he heard David yelling at Robert next door. He bolted across the yard and into the living room just as Robert grabbed Jerry's jacket and pulled the dazed boy to his feet. Robert drew his hand back for another blow.

"Bob, if you touch that boy, you won't live to go to prison!" Doug bellowed as he caught Robert's hand in mid-swing.

Robert froze in shock as he stared into Jerry's frightened face. Anger melted as shame overcame him. He lowered his fist and staggered to a chair. "I'm sorry Jerry," he sobbed, burying his head in his hands. "I didn't mean to hurt you. I know I let you down again. I'm sorry . . . I'm so sorry."

Doug was trembling with rage. "Bob, I'm taking Jerry home with me," he said through clenched teeth. "It'll take a court order for you to ever get him back. You drove your daughters away, but this boy stood by you no matter how you treated him. You are so stupid-blind drunk, you can't see what kind of boy he is, and how much he loves you."

Doug put his arm around Jerry, helping him toward the door. He took David's hand, pulling him to his feet. "Are you all right, Son?"

"Yeah, just a little short of wind. I'm sure glad you showed up when you did." David walked to Jerry's other side, and slipped his head under Jerry's arm. "You okay?"

Jerry blotted his bleeding lip with Doug's handkerchief and nodded, too choked to speak.

That night, Jerry cried himself to sleep while David's hand rested on his shoulder.

Suddenly, a gunshot pierced the night. Jerry bolted upright in bed. "Dad!" he screamed. Throwing off the quilt, he ran outside in David's pajamas, fear pounding wildly in his chest.

David and Doug were right behind him.

"No!" Doug grabbed him and held him in his arms. "You stay here with David. I'll check."

David hugged Jerry, feeling the horrible anguish and fear ripping through his thin body.

"No, Dad . . . oh please, no!" Jerry sobbed.

Jan ran up, wrapping her arms and a blanket around the boys. Jerry's sobs echoed in the cold night air as they waited, not even feeling the frost covered doorstep beneath their bare feet.

Doug appeared in the doorway, his face pale in the moonlight. Jan nodded, understanding his silence. She coaxed Jerry back to her warm living room, trying to shift his concern to his cold feet.

Jerry knew what had happened without being told. He'd stayed close to his father in spite of years of abuse because somehow, he'd always sensed it might end this way. He sat in the chair Jan led him to, motionless and numb with shock as she rubbed his icy toes. His body jerked when he heard the wailing of the sirens, but he didn't attempt to get up. He sat as though he was frozen, watching the red and blue lights dancing morbidly on the closed curtains.

An eternity passed. Then the lights vanished and Doug slowly walked into the living room. He looked at Jerry and sighed. "I'm sorry, Jerry . . ."

"I know," Jerry whispered, his face as expressionless as

stone. "Thanks for helping me." He rose on unsteady legs. "I'm really tired. Can I lay down?" The boys went to David's room, and Jerry collapsed on the bed.

"Jerry," David whispered, clasping his shoulder. "I just wish there was something I could do."

Jan slipped into the room and sat beside Jerry. She ran her fingers through his hair. "We love you very much, Jerry. We want you to know that you're like our own son. You can stay here with us as long as you want to."

Her touch, her fingers passing gently through his hair, reminded Jerry of his own mother. He rolled over and buried his face in the pillow, softly bleeding tears from deep within his broken heart.

Chapter 17

Now, twelve years later, the agony was still more than Jerry could bear. In the silence of the room, the haunting past crowded around him until he felt suffocated. He stood up and quickly left the hospital.

As he drove, the mood followed him home. He put his "open" sign in the gallery window, then paused shaking his head. "Not today," he groaned putting the "closed" sign back up. He entered the apartment and turned on the TV but the television couldn't drown out the gloom. *I think I'll take a long drive and get some fresh air*, Jerry thought, switching the set off.

He steered his van out of Slatersville and drove aimlessly up the highway. At the base of the mountain pass leading to Indian Valley, he pulled over and started to turn around. *What the heck*, he suddenly decided. *I need a friend right now, and Kimberly has been in Slatersville so much, she could probably use some help around her place.*

He made a full circle in the middle of the highway and started up the pass, hoping the fresh mountain air would blow the pain away like feathers in the wind.

When he reached Indian Valley, Jerry paused, judging the location of Kimberly's house by its proximity to David's cabin. He found a gravel road and turned in, following it to a driveway along the face of a hill. He pulled up to triple garage doors on the side of a large house cut into the hillside. Walking along a second story deck overlooking the lush pasture below, Jerry paused, gazing across the landscape. On the opposite side of the valley, he saw David's shake roof through the trees. Beyond that, the forest grew heavy, spreading into the foothills and up the rugged slopes of Thunder Mountain. Cochise and a black stallion grazed in the pasture that spread from Kimberly's ranch to the trees surrounding David's cabin. "What a view," Jerry said as he turned to knock on the double doors. Expecting to see Kimberly, he was startled when a slender young woman with smiling brown eyes and short, curly blond hair opened the door.

"Hi, can I help you?" she asked.

"I . . . uh . . . does Kimberly Dawson live here?"

"Jerry?" Kimberly came to the door. "What are you doing here? Is David okay?"

"Yeah, he's resting. He looks great, better than he did before the accident." Jerry broke into a grin. "He's mad though. He's starving and they won't give him solids until tomorrow. I wouldn't be surprised to see a nurse wearing Jell-O before breakfast. They're going to transfer him out of the intensive care unit today." Jerry shifted his feet. "I closed my shop early this afternoon. Guess everything was getting to me, so I went for a drive. Somehow I ended up here." He looked at Kimberly's guest. "Sorry, I should have called first." He smiled apologetically at Kimberly. "I've interrupted when you have company."

"Nonsense. Jerry, this is my cousin Roxanne Slater. She's been staying with me, so I don't have to drive alone to town everyday. She's your neighbor." Kimberly turned to Roxanne. "Jerry's my friend who runs the art shop behind your house."

Flashing Jerry a cheery smile, Roxanne extended her hand. "Hi Jerry, just call me Roxy." She winked at Kimberly. "You didn't tell me he was so handsome, Kim."

Wearing a self-conscious grin, Jerry took her hand. "Hi Roxy." He pushed his glasses up on his nose. "How is it we live so close, yet I've never seen you before?"

"You would have if I'd known *you* lived there." Roxanne laughed. "Kim and I took an extended vacation between semesters. Pity, we spent a whole summer touring Europe when I could have been getting acquainted with my new neighbor."

"Good grief, Roxy! At least let me invite him in before you start flirting." Kimberly took Jerry's other hand and pulled him inside. "Would you like a glass of lemonade?"

"Sure, if it's no trouble," Jerry answered, his eyes glued to Roxanne.

Kimberly smiled to herself and left to mix the lemonade.

"Please sit down," Roxanne pointed to a large overstuffed chair. As Jerry sat, she settled on the matching ottoman in front of him curling her bare feet under her. She smiled and a wrinkle creased the top of her small pug nose. Her dancing eyes lined with dark lashes locked with Jerry's as she leaned forward almost touching his knee. "So, tell me where you get all those gorgeous paintings I see hanging in your store windows. Do you paint, too?" Her smile was contagious, showing perfect white teeth. Her lips curved upward ending in dimples below her rosy cheeks. She wasn't a beautiful girl, but her features were most pleasing and pixie-like.

"No, I-I'm no artist," Jerry stammered. "I just sell the stuff. Most of my display is David's work. You know about David, don't you?"

Roxanne nodded. "It would be impossible not to. Kimberly talks of nothing else." Tenderness filled her eyes and she patted Jerry's hand. "Sounds like he had a close call. I'm glad he's better." Roxanne leaned her elbows on the knees of her jeans and rested her chin in her hands. She scrunched her face into a puzzled expression. "You know, it's strange. I've never seen Kimberly carry on so, especially about a guy she's barely met." She leaned closer, looking serious. "I'd bet my shiny new Porsche that she's falling in love."

Jerry nearly chuckled as Roxanne's appearance imprinted an image of Tinkerbell on his mind. He quickly looked away, composing himself with a phony cough. Laughter at that moment would be hard to explain.

The phone rang and Kimberly answered it. A moment later she hurried into the room, handed Jerry the glass of lemonade, and grabbed her purse and suede jacket. "A special order I placed just arrived, and I have to pick it up in Slatersville before five. I hate to run out on you, Jerry, but would you mind helping Roxy with my chores then take her home? I'll meet you later at the hospital."

"Be glad to," Jerry answered. His eagerness escaped his self-control with a goofy grin. What luck. Roxanne was fascinating; fate was giving him a perfect chance to get to know her better. Besides, something about her had melted his pain. He felt as carefree as a teenager, and a strange warmth grew in the pit of his stomach.

Roxanne seemed as pleased as Jerry. They rose and she hooked her arm through the crook of his elbow, flashing him a dazzling smile and leading him onto the deck. They descended the wooden staircase to the first floor patio, and then followed the path to the bottom of the terraced hill toward the barn, laughing and talking like old friends.

Realizing she was the one being left behind, Kimberly watched them as she walked along the deck toward the driveway. "Bye," she said, waving to herself. "I'm leaving now. Hope you don't mind." She giggled as she opened the garage, started the engine of her BMW, and steered toward town.

Chapter 18

David's nurse came into his room to disconnect the heart monitor and one of the IVs. "Congratulations," she said with a smile. "You're graduating from the intensive care unit. We're transferring you to a regular room."

"Good, does that mean I get regular food?" he asked with a grin.

"Persistent, aren't we?" The nurse chuckled, making a notation on his chart. "We wouldn't want to spoil you too much in one day."

"Please spoil me!" he rubbed his stomach. "Look at me. I'm wasting away. You don't want a dead patient on your conscience, do you? While you're writing, pretend you're the doctor, and order me some food! Deal?"

"No deal," she said, frowning at him over the top of her glasses with a twinkle in her eyes. "I'll get you some Jell-O."

"Tyrant." He pouted.

Once David was settled and alone in his new room, he turned his focus to his right-side weakness. Pushing the covers away, he elevated the head of his bed with the control. He bent and straightened his right knee several times, distressed at his inability to control his leg. Each time he tried to push his foot straight down, it slid awkwardly to the edge of the bed.

He reached to pull the sheet over him with his right hand, and the cover slipped off his numb fingers. Grunting in frustration, he attempted to make a fist, but he couldn't close his hand. Grasping his left forefinger, he squeezed it with all his strength, but succeeded in applying only slight pressure on his finger.

How am I going to paint? he thought as a surge of panic swept over him. *It'll take years to learn to paint with my left hand. My right hand feels like spaghetti. What if it never recovers? Mom's writing won't keep her, and my savings isn't that great. I have the Jeep and house payment. I don't have time to start over. Blast it! I can't afford to lose the use of this hand.* David rubbed his fingers, trying to push strength into them. He closed his eyes, struggling to force his hand closed while beads of cold sweat broke out on his forehead. Strained and breathing hard, he laid his head on the pillow. Suddenly, he sensed he was not alone and opened his eyes.

Kimberly was standing at the foot of his bed, a worried frown furrowing her brow. She held a paper sack and a large stuffed Appaloosa horse in her arms. "Are you all right, David?" she asked, setting her load on the bed and wiping his forehead with a washcloth.

David quickly pulled the sheet over his knobby knees with his left hand. He was stunned, speechless, and uncertain what to say if he could have found his voice.

"Don't push so hard. You've been through a terrible ordeal." She passed her fingers across his cheek. "You'll get better. Just give yourself some time." She smiled. "Jerry told me you were transferred, so I brought you a roommate." She handed David the horse.

David opened his mouth, but nothing came out. He managed a sheepish grin as he took the horse. Until this moment, Kimberly had seemed more like a dream. Now, finding himself fully conscious, he was completely unnerved by her presence.

Kimberly paused and smiled. David still stared at her in stupid silence. She babbled on, making him feel slightly less stupid. "I brought you something else. Jerry said you're starving today, but tomorrow you can eat anything in the house." She pulled a bowl from the sack and filled it with apples, oranges, bananas and grapes. "I brought you a start for breakfast. To keep out of trouble with your nurse, I'd better put this out of sight for now, though. Should I hide it in the closet?"

"Uh . . . no. Set it by the sink where I can see it," David finally stammered. He broke into a grin as he gathered self-control. "I can't reach it over there. They won't let me out of bed, but drooling over it will give me hope." He looked at the toy in his hand. "Thanks for the horse. Where did you find a stuffed Appaloosa?"

"I called in a rush order from a catalog at the novelty shop." She straightened some yarn strands of the horse's mane. "Cute, isn't' he?"

"He's great . . . thanks." David caught Kimberly's hand and pulled her closer. "Kimberly, I . . . I've been mostly out of touch with the real world since we met in that ravine." He stumbled over the words. "I feel at a disadvantage. So much that has happened is blank and cloudy. I remember you were there helping me. I'm aware that my condition was critical. I sensed on the way to the hospital that my life was in your hands. Thank you, Kimberly. Thank you for my life."

David looked away, fighting the emotion swelling inside him. He pressed her hand against his chest.

Kimberly swallowed hard, recalling the last time he'd held her hand. She leaned over and kissed his cheek. "I'm glad I was there. I'd wanted to meet you since that day at the pond, I just didn't expect our introduction to be so dramatic." She was quiet for a moment, then she tucked her other hand around David's right hand, gently caressing his weakened fingers. "Don't worry David," she said, her voice tender with compassion. "You'll paint again."

Her sensitivity to his worst unspoken fears released a reservoir of feelings. "Oh Kimberly, thank God you were there," he blurted out, reaching for her. She sat on the bed, leaning into his arms as he encircled her shoulders and pulled her to him. He clenched his jaw, checking his emotions as he buried his face in her hair. Breathing in her mild perfume, he just held her close. When he loosened his embrace and she sat upright, tears were welling up behind her lashes.

"My courageous little friend," he said, taking her chin in his hand and looking into the blue depths of her eyes. "By what wonderful miracle did you come into my life to help me and cry for me?" He drew her to him again in a tender embrace.

Just then, Jerry appeared in the doorway. "Hey, what's

this?" he said, grinning mischievously. "Dave, I didn't think you could move that fast. I see I was mistaken."

Kimberly quickly stood up and placed the stuffed horse on the windowsill where its juvenile face could smile at David.

"Kimberly, I understand you've met this clown," David said, flashing Jerry a phony look of irritation.

"Ah, yes, my friend." Jerry chuckled. "I held her in my arms before you did." His face became serious as he slipped his arm around Kimberly's shoulder. "She's one heck of a hero in my book. After some dim-wit I know tried to kill himself, this little lady hauled you off a mountain and watched over you all night. She stood by you for hours the next night while you teetered on the brink, holding your hand and encouraging you to hang on and keep fighting for your life."

"How did you know?" Kimberly stammered.

"The nurse told me. She thought you probably pulled David through that night."

David stared at Kimberly, moved by what he was hearing. He recalled her concern for him from his alarming collapse on her floor to fading moments in her car nearing Slatersville. Overwhelmed with awe and gratitude, he wondered at her devotion to him.

Kimberly busied herself rearranging the fruit basket, keenly aware of David's earnest gaze.

"Oops, I think my praise hath embarrassed the young maiden," Jerry teased. "She hath turned pink."

Kimberly felt the flush spreading across her face. "Oh stop it," she said, punching Jerry's arm as she escaped out the door. "I'm going to get a drink."

Jerry grabbed David's hand in a tight grip. "Hey Dave, this woman loves you. I can feel it in my bones. I know I'm right," Jerry insisted as Dave shook his head. "This isn't just a physical thing, although you two look like Apollo and Aphrodite. I'm talking the real eat, sleep, live with and get old and wrinkled together stuff. You know, its called M-a-r-r-i-a-g-e—that for time and forever thing people do."

"Calm down, Jerry," David said. "She hardly knows me."

"So what? I've been watching her. I've watched you, too, and I'm dead right. Face it Dave, you love the girl. You've always said you'd know the woman of your dreams when you saw her."

"Maybe you're right, Jerry, but cool down, and let it happen on its own, okay?"

"Whatever . . . but there's more to this than just blind fate. A greater hand is at work here."

Amazed at the firmness of Jerry's conviction, David felt a strange warmth tingle through him as truth embedded itself into his heart. He smiled and gave Jerry a push toward the door. "Well, if you're so determined to get us together, you'd better go find her. It was your big mouth that scared her away."

By evening, David's head hurt and he was exhausted, yet he hadn't wanted Jerry and Kimberly to leave. They coaxed him through his clear liquid supper, waking him so Kimberly could spoon-feed him the last few bites.

"I think we're finished. He's gone for the night," she said to Jerry as she wiped David's mouth. She lowered the head of his bed and covered him with the blanket. "Good night, David," she whispered, caressing his ear between her fingers. "I love you."

Jerry stood in the doorway watching David's quiet slumber. He'd been relieved with each stage of David's progress. Now he finally felt a sense of peace that all was well. Breathing a tired sigh, he followed Kimberly out of the hospital.

Chapter *19*

The following morning was discouraging for David. He was awakened by a miserable headache and his stomach was upset. *This is the pits,* he thought, eyeing his fruit basket. *Yesterday I was hungry enough to eat my stuffed horse, and they wouldn't feed me. Today I can finally eat, but I'd rather throw up.*

Following an EEG test to measure his brainwave activity, he refused breakfast, preferring instead to rest. An hour later, a physical therapist and a nurse woke him. "We need to get you up," the nurse said, helping David into pajama bottoms.

"Do I have to?" David asked. "I'd rather sleep off this headache."

"Sorry," the nurse said, "doctor's orders. Just while I make your bed, okay?' David shrugged and nodded as she placed a pair of hospital slippers on his feet.

They sat David upright and swung his feet over the edge of the bed in one easy movement. The action made his head throb and he felt dizzy.

"Whoa, let me lay down," he said grasping the nurse's hand.

"Dizziness is to be expected. Breathe deeply and the head rush should let up. Just sit still until you feel stable."

"I am stable," he complained. "It's the stupid room that won't hold still. Oh, my head hurts. Can I lay back down now?"

"I know it's hard David, but we need to get you moving."

David closed his eyes to block out the spinning room, and gradually the sensation began to subside.

The therapist gripped David's right arm. "All right," he said. "Stand up slow and easy."

With the nurse supporting David's left side, they helped him to his feet. He trembled, feeling weak and light-headed, but was determined to achieve it if it had to be done. His right leg felt numb, so he put his full weight on his left leg, but his body swayed. He felt fingers tightening on his arms.

"Just stand still until you get your balance."

David heard the words but he didn't know who said them. Somehow, he felt like he was outside of a dream, watching it from far away.

"Take a step forward," a distant voice instructed.

David obeyed, but his reaction was involuntary. The pain in his head became a steady roar, and pressure clouded his vision.

"His right leg can't support his weight," a voice warned. "David put your weight back on your left leg."

The ability to respond seemed as distant as the voice.

"We're losing him. Get him back to bed."

The room spun wildly as words echoed into nothingness, and David crumpled in their arms. They took his full weight, gently lowering him to the floor.

The nurse pushed the emergency call button and yelled, "We have a patient down in here! Bring a resuscitation bag. He's having trouble breathing." She grabbed an ammonia capsule from her pocket and burst it under David's nose, but he didn't respond. Seconds later, two nurses rushed into the room and helped lift David's limp body onto the bed.

"Hand me the ambu bag and call Dr. Jonston," the head nurse ordered. David's breathing was shallow and jerky. She placed the black mask over his face and assisted each breath as another nurse rushed to obey.

Moments later she returned. "Dr. Jonston's on his way. He wants the patient transferred back to the ICU stat!"

Chapter 20

Jerry rushed into the Intensive Care Unit. "What happened?" he cried. "They called and told me David's back over here."

"I'm sorry, Mr. Stone," Dr. Jonston answered. "We're not certain why, but he's had a serious setback. We've been monitoring some fluid build-up in his cranial cavity. It's been increasing through the night, but it hasn't been significant enough to cause this type of relapse. We're expecting to find some answers when we get the results of the X-rays. His condition is serious, but stable." The doctor pointed toward David's new room. "You can go in with him. I'm heading to X-ray to review the films with the radiologist."

Jerry stared in disbelief at David's still form attached to all the same tubes and wires. A respirator hissed oxygen into his lungs with each breath. It was like a terrible reoccurring nightmare. "This can't be happening," Jerry mumbled, weakly dropping into the chair as he pulled off his glasses. "I don't understand. He was getting better. I had such a good feeling about his progress."

A few moments later, Dr. Jonston hurried to the nurse's desk with a handful of X-rays. "I want the lab to run a type and cross match on a unit of blood for David Young stat! Call his mother for consent and prepare him for immediate surgery."

Praying silently in David's room, Jerry overheard the doctor and approached him. "What went wrong? Why do you have to operate again?"

"The fluid has increased considerably and needs to be drained. However, the critical problem seems to be a tiny bone fragment we missed due to bleeding and severe edema. The pressure of the fluid is pushing the bone deeper into the brain. It will have to be removed and the drain shunt inserted."

Jerry moaned as despair encompassed him.

Dr. Jonston gave Jerry's shoulder an encouraging squeeze. "Your friend made incredible progress before against some pretty tough odds," he stated. "I think this surgery will get him on a sound road to recovery."

Two hours later, Dr. Jonston met Jerry and Kimberly in the waiting room. "The surgery went well," he said, smiling broadly. "David is in recovery. I think the piece of bone we removed was causing his paralytic symptoms. We won't know until he's conscious how much improvement we'll see in his right-side function, but I'm very optimistic. He's stable, the shunt is draining, and his breathing is strong and steady."

Later in David's room, Jerry and Kimberly stood on either side of David, each holding one of his hands. The nurse worked around them, taking vital signs and adjusting the IV, then ignoring the one-visitor rule she smiled and left. Finally, David began to stir.

David slowly regained consciousness sensing soft pressure on his left hand and a firm, quivering grip on his right one. His eyelids flickered, then opened and his groggy stare focused on Kimberly. Her hair fell in graceful waves against her face and tumbled over her shoulders. Her eyes held David in their gaze with an expression of gentleness beyond his experience. She smiled, passing her fingers across his cheek and ear, letting them linger at the base of his neck. Deeply stirred, he lay in the warmth of her presence and caressing touch.

Jerry's voice drew David's attention from Kimberly. "Dave . . . are you . . ." his voice broke.

David turned, looking into Jerry's haggard face and managed a grateful smile. "You look terrible," he whispered.

Jerry gently embraced David's shoulders as tears flowed unashamed down his face. Jerry held David for a long moment as overwhelming relief swallowed the deep depression that had shrouded him all day. Finally he eased his stricken friend back onto the pillow. "Man, if you ever get reckless again, I swear I'll kill you," he choked, wiping his face and nose with his handkerchief. "You've made a nervous wreck out of me. Now quit messing around and get rid of that bed."

"Sounds like a plan," David mumbled, squeezing Jerry's palm.

Jerry's eyes swept to David's right hand. "It works," he said, grasping David's hand a little too tightly between both of his. "Thank God, you're gonna be okay."

David winced, then tightened his grip, rejoicing in new strength flowing through his fingers.

Turning back to Kimberly, David released Jerry, reaching up to brush away a tear that had spilled over her dark lashes. "Ghosts don't cry," he whispered.

She laughed, clasping his right hand and pressing it to her lips. "Thank you, dear Lord. I've always believed in miracles."

"Miracles . . ." David breathed a long tired sigh. "Like you." He closed his eyes as his body relaxed in sleep.

Jerry moved to the window and leaned heavily on the sill.

"You okay, Jerry?" Kimberly asked, hurrying over to him. Jerry nodded, turning to embrace her. He held her tightly. Then without speaking, he left the room.

Kimberly returned to David's side. While he lay resting in the healing power of slumber, a hint of ruddy color touched his pale cheeks. For the first time since Kimberly had watched this handsome young artist at work, she perceived the glow of life growing strong again within him.

The sweet warmth of the aura surrounding David had drawn her to him at the pond. That seemed so long ago. Now, unforeseen destiny had thrown them together, twisting their lives into an intimate closeness, which revealed itself like a spiritual awakening. "I love you, David," she whispered, running her fingers across his forehead. "I don't understand how it happened. Reason says it's too impetuous, too sudden. Oh, bother! Sometimes reason is for fools! The spirit may whisper like a silent breeze, but the truth it bears penetrates like a thunderbolt. All I need to know is that I love you."

Chapter 21

"David, the long awaited moment has arrived," the nurse said as she carried a steaming breakfast tray into David's room.

"I can't believe it. You're finally giving me food? Could you hand me that fruit basket too."

She started to set the basket on the table beside his tray.

"No, no. Right here." He put it beside him in bed like a greedy miser. "I'm not taking any chances. Food's been too hard to come by," he said, reaching for the fork on his tray before she wheeled the table in place.

After breakfast, David was transferred from the ICU. *What an awesome view*, he thought looking out the window of his new room. *Sometimes I wondered if I'd ever see another snow-capped mountain.* He picked up a banana, held it like a brush, and began painting the scene on the air. Suddenly, he dropped the fruit into his lap, watching his hand open and close as if he'd discovered a rare, priceless treasure.

Blinking back tears, his gaze followed the slopes of Buckskin Peak to where it touched the sky. "Thank you, God," he whispered pressing his hand to his heart. "Thank you."

Then in the quiet solitude of his room, David telephoned his mother. He tenderly consoled her as she sobbed, overjoyed at the sound of his voice. David talked to her for a long time, assuring her over and over that he was okay.

Several days later, the shunt was removed and David was discharged from the hospital. He bid his nurses a grateful farewell. Although he was thinner and weak after his ordeal, he walked to Kimberly's car and into Jerry's apartment without help. He rested on the couch while Jerry helped Kimberly prepare lunch. David's mouth watered as he breathed in the savory aroma floating from the kitchen. Finally, Jerry ushered him to the table.

"Ummm . . . this is the first home-cooked food I've tasted in an eternity," David said, gobbling down his first helping and reaching for seconds. He winked, flashing Kimberly a telltale smile. "You're going to make somebody's tummy happy when you get married."

Jerry nodded toward David. "Yeah, some guys get all the luck. Ow!" He winced when David's foot whacked his shin under the table. David cast a subtle frown in his direction and Jerry's grin turned silly. He quickly stuffed another bite into his mouth, stifling a snicker.

Kimberly noticed the clumsy exchange between the two men. Lightly blushing and giggling to herself, she stood and took her dishes to the sink, aware that Jerry was receiving a whispered lecture behind her back.

David stayed with Jerry for several days enjoying his company as he regained his strength. However, he was puzzled by Jerry's odd behavior. Each morning after breakfast, Jerry made certain David was comfortable, then he disappeared for over an hour. He returned whistling and cheerful to open the gallery at ten o'clock, but he never said a word about where he'd been.

David's curiosity was swelling, but he kept a lid on it, figuring that jerry would tell him when he was ready. Then one morning after opening the shop, Jerry bustled about the kitchen humming to himself. Suddenly, he laughed out loud.

David could stand the suspense no longer. He got up from his recliner and stood in the kitchen doorway, arms folded across his chest like a suspicious parent. "Okay Jerry, come clean. What are you up to? What is making you so all-fired happy? All this singing and whistling is driving me nuts."

Jerry tried to look serious and innocent. "I don't know what you're talking about. Just following my normal routine." But he couldn't suppress an idiotic grin. He pushed his glasses up onto his nose and cleared his throat as he quickly turned and stuffed some silverware into the dishwasher.

"Yeah, and I'm ten feet tall, about as tall as your story." David returned to his chair, irritated at himself for feeling offended that Jerry hadn't confided in him. He picked up the remote and switched on the TV, pouting in spite of himself.

"Hey Dave," Jerry sat on the coffee table in front of David and turned the television off. "I know we've always been open with each other. It's just that you've been the handsome hunk the girls swoon over. I've had my share of dates, but they usually fizzle out after the third or fourth time. I've just never met a girl before that I was crazy about who likes me back. I guess I was keeping quiet in case it doesn't work out."

David's eyes widened and a smile spread across his face. "A woman? You've been disappearing on me because you're seeing a woman? Jerry, that's great!"

Jerry's grin became more foolish and he lowered his eyes. "We go bike riding every morning before I open the shop. We're not getting serious or anything . . . not yet, anyway. We just have a lot of fun together."

"Who is she? When did you meet her?"

"She's Kimberly's cousin. They've both been helping me with the gallery while I visited you in the hospital."

"Oh really? Well, I think it's time I meet this woman who's got you acting like a half-witted teenager. You and Kimberly have kept this quiet long enough." David picked up the phone and punched the numbers Kimberly had given him. "Hey, Kimberly, David here . . . Sure, I'm fine. You said to call if I need anything. Are you free tonight? . . . Good, come over and fix dinner for me, okay? Jerry's cooking is killing me. Hey, bring your cousin, too. I don't know what she's done to Jerry, but she needs to put him back together . . . Good, we'll call it a date. See you at six." Grinning with self-satisfaction, David placed the receiver in its cradle.

Jerry, who had been frantically shaking his head, threw his arms in the air. "I knew I shouldn't have told you," he spouted. "Look at this place. I haven't touched it for days because some lamebrain took a stupid notion to go horseback riding in the middle of the night. Now you invite two women over without even asking me." He stormed into the kitchen, slamming dishes into the dishwasher while David relaxed in his chair, wearing a smug grin.

Jerry grumbled all day as he swept, mopped, and scrubbed the apartment, between waiting on customers. David watched with amusement. This was obviously more than a passing fancy. He had never seen Jerry so rattled. Six o'clock came and Jerry was as nervous as a sixteen-year-old going on his first date.

The doorbell rang and David went to greet their guests. His heart took a leap, then fluttered brainlessly in his chest when he saw Kimberly. Taking a deep breath, he tried not to let his giddiness show on the outside as he smiled and took a sack from her.

"Hi Kimberly, you can't imagine how good you and these groceries look after staring at Jerry's face for three days and eating his boxed dinners."

Kimberly smiled. "I hope I look better than the groceries. You're not very flattering."

David looked embarrassed.

"Oh, I know what you meant." She giggled as she stepped inside. "David, this is my cousin, Roxanne Slater."

Roxanne flashed David a wide smile and shook his hand. "Hi David, call me Roxy. I'm thrilled to finally meet you." Her sparkling brown eyes quickly assessed David, claiming him as a friend. Then she turned, looking for Jerry. She spotted him giving a final wipe to a cabinet and bounced through the kitchen doorway. Without hesitating, she hugged him, then took his hand and led him like a puppy into the living room. Gently pushing Jerry into a chair, she took the sack from David. "You guys get comfy, and do whatever guys do while Kimberly and I prepare to delight your bellies."

David was amused and a little taken back by this small blond whirlwind who had clearly bewitched Jerry with her delightful charm. He glanced at Kimberly.

She nodded and winked, saying without words what David had instantly realized. Roxanne was just the kind of woman Jerry needed. His nervousness had melted the moment she touched him. His deep blue eyes, in fact his entire persona, were glued to her with captive admiration. David hadn't seen his friend this happy since Jerry was ten years old. David smiled, feeling good about this bubbly, pretty woman who had the power to change Jerry's life. He hoped with all his heart that she would be the long-prayed-for healing balm to erase years of loneliness Jerry had endured.

Chapter 22

The days with Jerry had been restful and pleasant, but David was eager to return to his valley, his horse, and his cozy little cabin. Although he was still weak, David insisted on going home Monday.

"You're as foolhardy as you are stubborn, Dave," Jerry protested. "What's one more week going to hurt? Its not like Cochise is your baby or your house will collapse if you're not there to hold it up. I just don't think you should try to go it alone yet."

David grinned. "You're like an old mother hen, Jerry. Quit clucking. I'll be careful. I'm not totally incompetent."

"Well, that's debatable," Jerry said, walking David to Kimberly's car. "All I can say is a mule is a mule, and not likely to be anything else."

Kimberly listened to the friendly hassle chuckling to herself as she loaded David's belongings into her back seat.

Jerry hugged David. "Don't take any dumb risks, call Kimberly or me if you need help."

"Right," David answered clasping Jerry's hand in a firm grip. He couldn't say what he felt, so he just said, "Thanks for everything, Jerry." His eyes revealed the rest, and Jerry nodded his understanding.

"I'll miss your ugly face and constant complaining," Jerry chided. "Kimberly invited Roxy and me over this weekend, so I'll check on you Saturday."

David smiled and settled back in the seat as Kimberly steered toward Indian Valley. "I feel a lot different than I did the last time I traveled this road," he said.

"You look a lot different, too. You really had me scared."

"I was in good hands," he said, plucking her right

hand from the steering wheel and gently caressing her fingers. "Do you mind?"

She grew timid and a touch of redness crept into her cheeks. "No," she answered. "I guess it's your turn. I held your hand a lot in the hospital."

"Why?"

Kimberly glanced at David. He was looking at her with unwavering serious blue-gray eyes that seemed to penetrate deeply into her heart.

"Because I was worried about you. I thought it might help you to feel someone there with you."

"Is that the only reason?" he asked his steady gaze boring into her concealed feelings.

A brighter red flushed across her face. "David! You're putting me on the spot."

"I know, but I want an answer. You didn't just take care of me like a good neighbor or friend. It went far beyond that. All the hours you sat with me, stood by me, held my hand, waited, worried, prayed for me. Jerry told me all about it. Why?"

Kimberly hesitated, her mind searching for a way to escape his probing questions and disarming gaze. Then the intensity of the experience, the fear, the endless hours of worrying and waiting, all tumbled back into Kimberly's thoughts. Suddenly, she pulled to the side of the road and started to cry.

"I'm sorry," David said, surprised and confused as he gathered her in his arms. "I didn't mean to upset you."

All her reserve crumbled in his gentle embrace. "I was afraid for you, David. I was just so afraid . . . that I'd lose you when I'd barely found you. I . . . . I love you," she whispered.

David lifted her face toward him and his smile melted through her. "That's the 'why' I was hoping for."

Kimberly stared at him, hardly daring to believe.

David looked into her eyes, laying bare the tenderness in his soul. "Kimberly," he said, leaning closer to her, "I'm telling you that I love you too."

Kimberly was momentarily dazed. Then she threw her arms around his neck with a delighted squeal. "I knew this was meant to happen. I've felt it since the first time I saw you."

David winced as her impulsive hug jolted him.

"Oh, I'm sorry." She drew away.

"Kimmy, I'm all right," David said, pulling her to him. He cradled her in his arms and softly kissed her.

When their lips parted, Kimberly felt warm tingles passing through to her toes. She snuggled against David, laying her head on his shoulder and sighed. *Thank you God, thank you for setting our feet on unknown paths. Thank you for making me wait for blessings I've yet to realize so I will be more humble and grateful. Thank you for letting me know David, and for granting all I've ever dreamed of and hoped for.*

Finally, she sat up, running her fingers across his smooth-shaved cheek. "I'd better get you home. Try to rest for awhile." She lowered his seat, placing a pillow under his head, and steered onto the highway. Then she slipped her hand into David's.

Relaxing in the seat, he closed his eyes as infinite thoughts and desires flowed through his mind. Kimberly was the center of them all. He smiled, letting her touch and presence fill him with warmth.

Suddenly, David sat upright. He took her hand in both of his and looked at her intently. "You will marry me, won't you?"

Kimberly pulled to the side of the road again. "Is this a proposal, David?"

Startled by his own impulsive question, David wanted to kick himself. "Guess I didn't pick the most romantic setting, did I?" he mumbled, staring at her small fingers entwined with his own. "I . . . it just came out."

Kimberly's eyes sparkled with happiness. "I think the setting is perfect, David." She smiled, taking a deep breath as she placed her other hand over his. "I'm very honored, and I accept with all my heart."

A thrill passed through David, taking away his breath. He drew Kimberly to him, and kissed her more fervently. Then he held her tight. The events that had taken place in the past few weeks seemed like a painful dream. Now, bringing exquisite happiness, the dream had become wondrously sweet. Nothing could ever be the same. His arms were holding a beautiful miracle. She was alive, cherished, and loved as though he'd known her forever. It was so incredible he feared he might wake up and find it was only a dream. Holding her close reassured him as she nestled warm against his chest.

Finally, she pulled away. "David, I have to get you home. Please try to rest."

David lay quiet for some time as Kimberly drove up the winding pass. Suddenly, he raised his seat upright. "How did you disappear at the cliff? And don't tell me your horse climbed a tree."

Kimberly gave David a startled glance. "What in the world are you talking about?"

"Early in the morning the same day I saw you at the pond, your horse galloped past me on the hill behind my place. I wanted to meet you, so I followed you, but you vanished at the base of the cliff."

"Oh that." A touch of mischief twinkled in her eyes. "Actually, it was a large tree, and he's a very talented horse." She couldn't restrain a snicker as he frowned at her. "I'm sorry, David," she said, forcing herself to be serious. "Really, I had no idea I was stressing someone into thinking I was a ghost. It's no wonder when you were hurt and confused, you mistook me for Aunt Marnie."

Kimberly grew quiet, a look of melancholy in her eyes.

"I gather it's a secret you can't discuss," David probed, feeling uneasy about her sudden change of mood.

"Just sweet reminiscing," she answered. "It is a secret, the only one my father ever had." She paused, deep in thought. "He would have liked you, David Young." She glanced at David and smiled, but her eyes were sad. "He would want me to share with my sweetheart. I wish he could have been here to show it to you.

"There's a narrow ravine hidden by the underbrush. It descends into a crevice behind the cliff where a stream tumbles through the canyon and over a waterfall into Blue Lake. It's quite spectacular. My parents and I used to picnic there, but mostly Dad and I loved to fish. At one point, the stream widens into a deep pool. Since it's so isolated, the trout in it are as big as cows. Dad and I were the envy of every angler in the valley. Dad found the ravine by accident when a rattlesnake spooked his horse and he was thrown off into the crevice. He limped home, wearing the smile of a conqueror, announcing that it was his lucky day. Horses were our livelihood and we loved them, but fishing in our secret spot was our favorite pastime. We built a lot of memories there, David . . . I miss him."

"I understand." David nodded, remembering his own father with a wave of loneliness. He thought it interesting that the one form of recreation he and Doug Young had avoided was the kind Kimberly and her father had enjoyed the most. "Thanks for sharing," David said, smoothing a strand of hair away from her face.

"As soon as you're well, I'll take you there," she said.

A sudden thought sparked an impish gleam in David's eyes. "Hey, since you're a pro, maybe you can teach me to catch something besides minnows. Man, would that blow Jerry away. I can see him now, ranting that we always catch bigger fish than he does, and begging us to share our secret. After years of his taunting, that would be sweet revenge."

"You'll get it," Kimberly promised. "Now, will you please try to rest? The hardest part of the trip is still ahead."

David laid back in his seat, chuckling to himself.

By the time they reached Indian Valley, the twisting road had taken its toll on David. His face was pale and his head throbbed. Kimberly drove him to her house, insisting that he shouldn't go home until he was stronger. She threatened to return him to Jerry if he argued.

He sensed that she was right and agreed. Kimberly took David to the same room he'd awakened in after his accident, and he lay down, welcoming the soft bed. Kimberly pulled off his boots and socks and tucked the quilt over him. David humbly accepted her help. She gave him a drink of juice and a pain pill, and then sat on the bed beside him, rubbing the tautness in the back of his neck. Eased by the gentle caress of her fingers, David moaned softly as her touch soothed and relaxed him to sleep. He slept all afternoon and through the night.

Chapter 23

David woke as sunlight danced through the window. He remembered his first awakening in the same bed and sighed with relief. A supper tray was sitting on the table beside the bed, the words "I love you" written on the napkin beneath a red rose. David picked up the rose and sniffed its sweet fragrance, then laid it on the table in front of an old photograph.

Suddenly, he recalled the picture of the Slater family and looked directly into the sad face of Marnie Slater. He started, taken back at the amazing resemblance between the woman and Kimberly. Memories of dreams flashed across his mind and sent a tingle up his spine. David looked away. It was foolish to allow those feelings to return, yet there was something about her eyes that was too familiar. David denied the thought, and the ghostly legend succumbed to the existence of a real person who had lived and died, her tragic story forever unfinished.

David sat up and looked around. Kimberly lay sleeping on the Victorian sofa, snuggled beneath a comforter. A vast stirring of devotion never before imagined swelled inside him as he watched her quiet breathing. He studied her features, still trying to grasp the reality of their future together. *Oh my sweet Kimmy*, he thought, folding his arms across his chest. *In this great big world, how was I so blessed to move into your little corner of it? It's been a month of miracles that's for sure.*

Kimberly stirred and opened her eyes. She blinked a few times, then smiled and sat up, smoothing her hair. "Morning, David. You slept so long I thought I gave you an overdose. Feeling better?"

"Thanks to you," he answered enjoying her slightly rumpled appearance. "Come here and tell me I didn't just dream yesterday."

Kimberly sat on his bed, leaning against him as he wrapped

his arms around her. "If you did, it was my dream too."

"I'll make it official as soon as I can get to town and buy my girl a diamond," he said, hugging her to him and kissing the top of her head.

"I've already got one." She turned and kissed him. They lingered in an embrace, then she stood up to pick up the supper tray. "I'll get you some breakfast."

David caught her hands, placing them on his temples. "Don't need food, just you and your gentle touch." He wrinkled his face. "Rub there . . . ah yes." David smiled to himself. "My neck, Honey . . . umm . . . shoulders too." He closed his eyes, soaking up the pleasant sensations flowing through her fingers.

A frown furrowed her brow. "Are you okay?" she asked.

"Couldn't feel better," he said with a grin.

Kimberly's hands dropped to her hips. "That was sneaky," she scolded. "You're goofing off while I'm thinking you're in pain."

"If I say I am, will you do it again?"

She tossed her head and picked up the tray. "Soggy corn flakes sound like a good breakfast for a smart aleck," she said as she left the room.

David chuckled and climbed out of bed, but his smile faded as his gaze was drawn again to the picture of Marnie Slater. Her eyes . . . something about her eyes sent a queer shiver through him. Shaking his head, he picked up the rose and the photograph, and carried them into the large country kitchen.

Kimberly was cracking eggs into a blender. David slipped up behind her, encircling her waist with his arms and kissed her cheek. She jumped, nearly dropping an egg.

"David, you scared me! I thought you were still in bed. Don't sneak up like that." She leaned against him, taking pleasure in the comfort of his arms.

"I didn't sneak. You hid my boots. Can't help it if feet don't make noise."

"Well, take your feet and sit down so I can cook!"

David obediently sat on the snack bar, smelling the rose.

"Thanks for the note and the flower. I think it needs a little water though."

Kimberly looked at David sitting on her cabinet, his bare feet dangling, his head wrapped in gauze, and the wilted rose twirling between his fingers. She suddenly burst into laughter. Was this the same handsome intrepid artist she'd longed to meet at the pond? Yet her feelings for him had grown far beyond anything she had imagined then.

"What's so funny?" he asked indignantly.

"Just happy," she answered, cracking another egg.

"Humph!" he grunted, feigning hurt. "Sounded more like laughter at a circus clown. Remember, I'm wounded, so you have to be nice to me."

"I'm sorry." Kimberly giggled and dumped the blended mixture into the frying pan.

David's eyes returned to the photograph. "Tell me about Marnie. I can't get over how much she looks like you."

"Neither could great Aunt Effie," Kimberly said. "She was only seven when Marnie died, and I guess she never felt at peace until I was born. She insisted I was sent as an omen. She believed there was a special bond between Marnie and me, like she was my guardian angel or something." Kimberly flipped the omelet over in the skillet. "I really can't tell you much, except what Aunt Effie told me. Effie was in her nineties when she died. She was a sweet, eccentric old lady, tough as nails, and as clear-minded as we are, but she only had her childhood memories. The family wasn't allowed to talk about Aunt Marnie."

Kimberly moved a strand of hair away from her face and smiled. "I do have a keepsake of Aunt Marnie. That cedar chest in your room and all its contents belonged to her. I inherited it when Aunt Effie died."

"Where did the ghost story come from?" David asked, leaning forward with interest.

"Somebody's imagination," Kimberly said with a shrug. "People fantasize about unsolved mysteries." She shook her head. "The whole tragedy was unnecessary. That's why it's so sad. If Grandfather Jacob hadn't been so haughty and stubborn, Marnie could have married the man she loved."

Kimberly glanced at David as she flipped the omelet onto the plates. He was watching her, his intense steady gaze boring though her. "David, why are you staring at me?"

"Are you free today? I have to do something."

"Like what?" She eyed him suspiciously. "Your doctor said to take it easy for at least three or four more weeks. Jerry warned me I'd have to tie you down to keep you out of mischief."

"Jerry's a pickle. If he didn't have someone's crisis to worry about, he'd go find one. I have to follow a creative impulse while its fresh. Please take me home right now."

Kimberly set the plates on the table, cocking her head to one side and pointing to the food. "Can we at least eat first?"

"Oh, sure. This looks terrific," he said with an embarrassed grin as he held her chair. "Sorry, I get a little carried away sometimes."

As David walked past his Jeep to get his paints, he stopped and scowled at the birds in his fir tree. "Look what you've done, you turdy-birds. Did you have to use my 'wheels' for target practice?" David flicked some bird manure from the shiny surface and began pulling his shirttail out of his jeans. He paused, and then broke into a grin and stuffed his shirt back in his pants. "Aw, forget it, I suppose even birds need some form of artistic expression. It's only a Jeep. It'll wash."

Soon David sat facing his pond with a large canvas in front of him and paints in his lap. Kimberly was stretched out on a blanket beside the shore with a book.

Grasping a paintbrush in his fingers, David studied his hand while tears welled up in his eyes. "Thank you God," he whispered, gazing upward. Then he smiled and began to paint.

"I hoped I could watch you work sometime," Kimberly said.

"I think you already did once," David teased with a wink.

"Guilty," Kimberly said, ducking her head behind her book.

"I mean when I'm not hiding in bushes." She peeked over the cover.

"You can't see this painting until it's finished. It's a surprise."

"How long will it take?" she asked.

His eyes were mischievous. "Dunno . . . days, weeks, months."

"That's not fair. I'll suffocate with curiosity."

"No problem, I know CPR," he said chuckling to himself. "I'll revive you when it's done."

Kimberly stuck her bottom lip out, trying on a pout. "Maybe I'll just feed you hot dogs tonight instead of the surprise I was planning."

He laughed. "Are you trying to bribe me? Sorry, won't work. I love hot dogs."

David painted rapidly with a wonderful creative power he'd never experienced before. Each stroke of his brush was precise and perfect as he felt strength flowing through his hand and onto the canvas.

Kimberly sensed the mood and was awed by David's intensity as he became one with his creation. She felt overjoyed at his depth of artistic spirit, so recently threatened by crushing disability.

David worked for hours. Finally, he leaned back to inspect his painting. He smiled, nodding with satisfaction. Stretching a kink in his neck, he sighed as he lay on the blanket beside Kimberly and closed his eyes.

"You push yourself too hard," she said, rubbing the knot in his neck.

"The work is healing. You have no idea how exhilarating it felt. My muscles are stiff so I'll quit, but I can't wait until tomorrow. I've never felt so inspired before." He sat up and gazed at the pond. "Everywhere I look, I see beauty and gifts I've taken for granted. It's like I'm seeing for the first time in my life. I realize now what's really important." He stood up, reaching for her hand. "Come on Honey, let's go home."

That night after Kimberly had gone to bed, David put on his

pajamas and climbed into his bed, but he was too excited to sleep. It seemed all his dreams were falling neatly into place as though directed by some unseen hand. He stared out the window at the millions of stars, comparing them with blessings, then got up and flipped on the light.

As he strolled in the bedroom, his toe caught on a strand of yarn in the hand-woven rug, and it began to unravel. David sat on the old cedar chest to unwind the yarn. The aging wood groaned, and something cracked. Fearing he'd harmed the treasured keepsake, David quickly stood up, lifted the lid, and inspected it for damage. It seemed intact. The contents were covered with a silk quilt. He lifted the quilt to see if anything had broken underneath.

David gasped as his eyes rested upon a familiar white gown lying in the chest. He picked up a corner of the gown, and it fell open to his view. He dropped it as though he'd been bitten. A picture slipped from the folds of the quilt and crashed to the floor. David stood frozen, still staring at the gown. Then he stooped to pick up the broken frame, turning it over to see if the photograph was damaged. The color drained from his face. Icy fingers of shock gripped him as he stumbled to the bed and sat down, the picture still clutched in his hand.

Chapter 24

Kimberly burst into David's room tying the belt to her robe. "David, what happened? I heard a loud crash." She hurried to his side and the photograph caught her eye. "Marnie and Nathan," she whispered. "I've never seen this before. Where did you find it?"

"My foot caught on some strands of carpet. I sat on the chest to unwind it. Something inside the chest cracked, so I opened the lid to see what I'd broken. This fell out of the quilt." David handed Kimberly the yellowing picture of a young man in humble dress clothes. He was sitting in a wooden chair with Marnie standing beside him, her hand resting on his shoulder. She was smiling and beautiful, wearing the same gown that lay on the floor where David had dropped it.

"Nathan's the stable boy?" David asked. His voice was a raspy whisper.

Kimberly nodded. "David, what's wrong? Why are you so upset?"

"That dress." There was a tremor in his hand as he pointed to the crumpled gown. "I've seen it before in my dreams."

Kimberly laid the broken picture on the bedside table. "David, you'd better lie down."

"The dreams . . . were so real like there was a message in them," David mumbled as she helped him into bed. "I'd forgotten that, but there was something so familiar about her eyes in the picture." He grasped Kimberly's hand. "I thought I'd been dreaming about you . . . but it was Marnie. She always stood beside the pond crying . . . and she was always wearing that gown.

Kimberly shook her head. "This is really strange. Your dreams . . . the picture." She stared at the old photograph. "How could I have overlooked it? I've gone through that trunk a dozen times. I'm sure I unfolded the quilt once. I found a locket with Nathan's picture in a jewelry box, but I've never seen this photograph." She stood in silent awe for some time. Finally she spoke. "Would you like to sleep in my room, David? I can stay in here."

"No . . . I'm a little shaken up, but I'm fine. Just confused. Why me? I was a stranger. Was she trying to warn me? There's more to it than that . . . What was she trying to tell me?" He settled his head on the pillow. "I wish I knew what it all means."

Kimberly shook her head as she ran her hand across David's brow. "Try to rest David." She kissed his cheek. Then, lost in thought, she turned and left the room.

Pale streams of moonlight filtered through the lace curtains as David finally drifted off to sleep. He slept fitfully, moaning and tossing. Finally toward morning, he settled into quiet, restful slumber.

When he awakened, his gauze turban was loose, so he unwound it. "Yuck," he said, looking in the dresser mirror at his remaining shaggy hair that had not been shaved from the top and sides of his head. He ran his fingers through the unruly mop.

Kimberly appeared, looking tired and a little pale. "Want a haircut?" she smiled, leaning against the door frame.

"Sure, if you're a barber," he answered.

"I'm no barber, but I'm good. I've trimmed horses for years."

David frowned at her.

She giggled. "I cut Dad's hair too." Then Kimberly's face grew serious, and she watched David for a moment. "Are you all right this morning?"

He nodded. "Yeah, all this has been unsettling, and I have a lot of questions, but I'm okay." He patted the bed beside him. "Come here, Kim. I want to hold you."

She sat beside him, and he slipped his arm around her shoulder. "I think I'm beginning to understand," he said, resting his cheek against her head. "Effie was right. Marnie must be very close to you. I dreamed about her again."

"You did?"

"I was taken back to my critical time in the hospital. You were crying and holding my hand. Marnie appeared in the room. She was crying too, but . . . her tears weren't for me. She grasped my other hand as the room faded, and we all seemed to be surrounded by clouds. I saw my father coming toward us. He reached for me . . ." David paused and swallowed hard. "I wanted so badly to take hold of his hand, but Marnie wouldn't let me go. She shook her head and seemed to be talking to someone. My father stood nearby for a long time. Then he smiled and waved as clouds surrounded him, and I couldn't see him anymore." David's voice choked, and he paused again. "After my father left, Marnie touched my forehead and smiled. Then she walked around my bed and embraced you."

David wrapped Kimberly in his arms. "Kim, it wasn't just a dream. It was more like . . . a vision. Maybe all of the dreams were visions. I believe Marnie asked God to let me come back to you." David buried his face in Kimberly's hair and closed his eyes tightly as a wave of emotion sent a tremor through his body. "I'm so grateful to be alive," he whispered.

David wasn't supposed to get his head wet, but the state of his hair was depressing. Careful to avoid the incision, Kimberly shampooed the top and sides of his head. After breakfast, she trimmed his hair while he supervised using a hand mirror. She finished and stepped back to inspect her job, feeling a warm thrill as she looked at the man she loved. The shaved area on the back of his head was beginning to grow back, and the rest of his sandy hair waved across his forehead and behind his ears. His soft steel-blue eyes twinkled. He looked robust and dashingly handsome.

"Kimberly, you're staring. Do I really look that good?" he joked.

"Yes," she answered, smiling and turning a little red. He winked at her and took her by the hand. "Let's go paint," he said, grabbing her car keys and leading her to the door. "I'm ready to create a masterpiece."

David worked each day with increased fervor and energy. Late Friday afternoon he set his paints down and leaned back in the lawn chair. "It's finished," he said with a long sigh. "I can't believe it. This is the best work I've ever done. Come here, Kim. You can see it now."

Kimberly arose from the blanket and moved to David's side. As he sat her on his knees, she looked at the canvas, sucking in a startled breath. "Oh David," she whispered.

With remarkable skill and inspiration, he had turned the canvas into an exquisite vision of her beloved pond. Surrounded by forest greenery so life-like that it appeared three-dimensional, the water was luminescent like silver-blue glass.

Kimberly's eyes were drawn to her own image in the foreground. Dressed in blue jeans and a yellow blouse, she was lying on her side leaning on one elbow with her chin resting in her hand. Long auburn hair fell across her shoulder to lay in soft curls on the ground. Her eyes focused on her book and a faint smile accented the lovely lines of her face. Kimberly read the neat scripting in the lower right hand corner; "All my dreams are fulfilled in you. Love Forever, David."

Kimberly immersed herself in the beauty of the painting, unable to find words. Finally, she stammered. "It . . . it's breathtaking, David. The pond is so alive, yet mystical like a fairytale suspended in time. How did you capture such a wonderful mood?"

"I painted it the way I saw it in my dreams. It's only background, though. Without your image, the painting wouldn't come to life." David rested his head on her shoulder and wrapped his arms around her waist. "Without you, I wouldn't be alive."

Kimberly caressed his hands. "Is that how beautiful you really see me, David?"

"No," he answered. "That's how beautiful you really are."

Kimberly turned around dangling her knees over the arm of his lawn chair, and put her arms around his neck. "I love you," she said, her eyes dancing with excitement. "Let's get married as soon as you're well enough to travel."

David grinned. "I was thinking the same thing."

Kimberly's smile was radiant. "I'll call Mom and tell her to pack her bags. She's finally getting the son she always wanted. She'll adore you."

"I just hope she *likes* me. Hey, we can celebrate with Roxy and Jerry tomorrow. Man, will this blow Jerry away. He's the impulsive one," David chuckled. "I told him to ease up and give us time to get to know each other."

"We are moving pretty fast," Kimberly said, curling David's hair around her finger. Then she hugged him. "Nothing I've ever done has felt more right though. We'll just have to discover each other as we grow together."

"A new adventure every day, huh?" David grinned.

Suddenly, Kimberly sat upright. "David, I've got a great idea. Let's move your mom into your cabin. You said she loves to fish. She could go fishing every day at the pond. My mom is so far away, and I always wanted my babies to have a grandma close who could spoil them. With your work and my inheritance, we can hire a nurse and Medical Air Transport could supply any of her other medical needs. In fact, I've seriously considered learning to fly. Especially after you got hurt. We could buy our own little helicopter. You and Jerry could distribute paintings more easily too. Will you think about it?"

Listening with delight to Kimberly's enthusiasm, David laughed. "I *am* thinking," he said. "We aren't even married yet, and we already have babies and a helicopter." He drew her close and wrapped her in his arms. "Oh Kim, we have an eternity for dreams. Right now, I just want to hold you."

She grew quiet, snuggling against his chest, and her closeness embraced his soul. He looked about. The world was magnificent. Sunlight bathed the rugged slopes of the mountains and the mingled scents of wildflowers floating from the foothills sweetened the summer breeze. Birds on graceful wings fluttered through the sky. The reflection of lazy clouds drifted on the surface of the pond.

David felt more alive and vibrant than he ever had before. He took a deep breath of the fresh mountain air, feasting on the pungent smell of pine needles. He was filled with the power and joy of life. He could walk on two good legs, and he could paint with marvelous new depth and inspiration. His future, bright, lovely, and cherished, was cradled against his heart.

David raised Kimberly's chin upward and softly caressed her lips with his. When their lips parted, his mouth curled in a smile and his eyes spoke his tender love.

Kimberly felt his arms, strong, yet so gentle against her. She felt the steady rise and fall of his chest and the soft moan of contentment passing through him. She gazed long and intently at David's handsome slender features. Wisps of sandy hair waved across his forehead and his alluring eyes kindled a stirring deep within her.

David winked with a mischievous, boyish grin. "Kimmy, you're staring again. I love being admired by those big beautiful sapphire eyes," he teased, "but I thought you had an important phone call to make." He slipped his hand under her knees and stood up, lifting her in his arms. "Come on little bride, let's go plan our wedding." David held her for a moment then set her down and took her hand in his.

As Kimberly and David left the pond, a soft breeze rustled through the quaking aspen and pine trees, stirring the leaves and branches. Gentle ripples on the water softly licked the shore. Suddenly, the pond grew calm and strangely luminous, like a polished mirror. The reflection of the trees seemed frozen and clouds hung motionless on the surface of the pond like a silent painting on silver-blue canvas.

The image of a woman with auburn hair covering her shoulders rested on the water. She lay elegant and beautiful, her white gown flowing against the stillness of the pond. Her face portrayed deep sorrow. Yet, as she watched David and Kimberly walking away, she smiled through her tears. An expression of pride radiated from her eyes while her faint whisper of hope was swallowed by the breeze. Holding David and Kimberly in her gentle gaze, she slowly raised her arms as though she was releasing a beloved bird to soar on wings of freedom.

Kimberly paused for a moment, sensing a strange lonely melancholy, but the feeling fled as suddenly as it had come. She felt warmed by a comforting spirit of peace as she proceeded up the path where David waited for her.

The pond remained beautiful and translucent for some time as the vision lingered like a masterpiece upon the crystal surface. The spirit's presence filled the hauntingly sweet aura surrounding the pond. Then Marnie's image drifted into shimmering ripples as the breeze swept across the water.

PART II

Chapter 25

Kimberly shivered and pulled her jacket more tightly around her as she leaned against the railing on the deck. Looking across the widening expanse of gray ocean, she could feel the cold mist floating upward from the wake behind the ferry. The Vancouver Island skyline gradually faded until it was swallowed by the rolling sea.

David stood beside Kimberly, his brow troubled, and confusion in his eyes. Finally he turned toward her placing his hand on her shoulder. "Kim, please tell me what's really bothering you. Is it something I've said or done? I'm sorry about the hassle over your luggage, the taxi problem, and the mad rush to catch the ferry, but we got here in time. You have enough clothes in your other bag for a few days. Then if your luggage doesn't catch us by the time we get to Skagway Saturday morning, we'll just buy you some new clothes. Now, is it still all that bad?'

Kimberly's bottom lip quivered. "It's so closed in down there," she murmured "Without a porthole, I can't see the ocean, and it's too cold to stay out here very long." She paused. "I just . . . well, I don't understand why you didn't make reservations for a nicer ferry. It's not like we couldn't afford it." Suddenly, she spun about, scowling at David. "That dinky cabin doesn't even have a double bed. Why didn't you reserve the larger cabin? At least we'd have our own bathroom."

"Kimberly, I'm sorry. I honestly didn't know. The larger cabins have four single berths." He lifted her chin, gazing repentingly into her tear-filled eyes. "I thought two would be more cozy for us. I never dreamed we'd have to go down the hall to the bathroom." Trying to find a lighter side to the situation, David put on a guilty grin. "Look at it this way, Honey, since the day we met our lives have been one crazy adventure."

He raised his hands in a futile gesture. "What else could possibly go wrong? Anyway, I'll make you a deal. I promise I'll put the money we saved on a smaller ferry into a savings account for your helicopter and flight training. When you get your license, we'll drop everything, and you can take me anywhere you want for the most romantic night you've ever imagined."

Kimberly turned back toward the ocean. "I'd kind of imagined that would be tonight, David. Now I don't even have a nightgown, and we're stuck for four nights in separate beds. I'm sorry, but I'm not in the mood for crazy adventures. Somehow, I had the impression we were going on a honeymoon."

David turned her around, drawing her to him. "I promise this will be a wonderful honeymoon, Sweetheart. We'll just share a bunk. We can't sleep any cozier than that. I know you had something special you wanted to wear for our wedding night, but no nightgown could make you more beautiful than you are. You'll look just as pretty in a pair of my pajamas." He gently pressed his lips against hers and her tenseness relaxed as she responded to his warming embrace.

David took her hand in his, turning the sparkling set of rings on her finger. He smiled at his own gold and diamond wedding band as he placed his other hand around her shoulder. "Come on Honey, let's imagine our own candlelight and have a romantic dinner before the cafeteria closes."

Kimberly's lips curled into a smile, and she blinked back her tears. Slipping her arm around his waist, she felt a sweet bond of intimate closeness. *It'll work out okay*, she thought while they strolled to the cafeteria. *We're together. Nothing else really matters.*

The following morning, David awoke to wondrous new sensations. Kimberly lay snuggled against him in the narrow bunk. He peered down at his sleeping wife, feeling a warm delightful sense of belonging to one another. Her lovely face, surrounded by tangled waves of auburn hair, lay against his chest, her head resting on his arm. She was adorable and child-like in his blue-and-white striped pajama top with the tips of her fingers barely peeking out of the long sleeve. He could almost see a teddy bear cuddled in the crook of her arm. She was his to cherish and care for. He must protect her always. David held her slender body against his own, awed by the splendid thrill passing through him. The sublime oneness he had shared with her during their wedding night was still burning within him.

The memory of his mother's pleasant voice reading a passage from her old and worn family Bible came to David's mind with a spirit of fresh understanding. "Therefore shall a man leave his father and his mother and shall cleave unto his wife and they shall be one flesh."

Four glorious days later, Kimberly and David gathered their luggage as the ferry pulled up to the pier in Skagway, Alaska. A firm tap sounded on their cabin door.

"Good morning sir," the purser said, snapping to attention when David opened the door. "We received a message that your lost luggage has arrived in Skagway."

Kimberly pushed past David. "My luggage made it?"

"Yes ma'am, they're holding it at a small air terminal." He gave her a piece of paper with the address.

"That's terrific," Kimberly said, pressing a ten-dollar bill into the purser's hand as he turned to leave. "Thank you."

"Ten dollars for a message?" David asked as he closed the door. "Are we really that grateful?"

"It was the smallest bill I had," Kimberly said. "Anyway, I thought you'd prefer he get money than the hug I almost gave him for that 'message.' I haven't been looking forward to a shopping spree in some quaint Alaskan village."

"Whatever," David shrugged with a grin. "But I had a five I could have given him, and you'd be five dollars closer to your wings."

David and Kimberly disembarked the ferry, admiring the

jagged mountains that surround Skagway. The granite slopes were barren and forbidding above the low timberline. A pleasant-faced Athabaskan Indian waited near the dock, holding open the door of a shuttle van. He deposited their bags in the rear, and drove David and Kimberly to the airstrip to claim her luggage.

As they returned from the airport, their chauffeur eagerly discussed points of interest as he drove down Skagway's famous Broadway Street. David and Kimberly felt they had somehow driven back through the gates of time. The rustic village, home of the Klondike Gold Rush National Historical Park, echoed the mood of the gold rush era from a remarkable array of original shops, boarding houses, and saloons.

After registering and securing their luggage at an aging hotel, David and Kimberly walked down the boardwalk to the railroad depot, the starting point for a walking tour of the preserved and restored Historical District.

When they returned to the hotel several hours later, Kimberly plopped onto the double bed and pulled off her sneakers and socks. "My feet are killing me," she groaned. " But I've never seen a town with such a colorful history or so many fascinating exhibits."

David filled two glasses with water. "Maybe we should plan to stay here longer and take in more of the sights," he said, handing her a glass. He propped a pillow against the headboard and leaned against it, stretching his long legs toward the foot of the bed.

Kimberly drained her glass and set it down. "You want my feet to fall off before we leave Alaska, don't you?" she chided, crossing her ankles in front of her and rubbing her toes and heels. "Besides, you've already got three more weeks so full of plans they'll probably burst." She sighed, gazing out the window. Then her brow wrinkled, and she grew unusually quiet and thoughtful.

"Something on your mind besides your feet?" David asked, curious about her sudden change of mood. Kimberly didn't answer, but continued to stare out the window, a distant expression in her large blue eyes. David frowned, gently placing his hand on her shoulder. "Kim, what is it?'

She glanced at him for a moment, seeming rather puzzled, then her attention was drawn back to the window. "It feels odd being here, realizing a part of my family's history took place in the Alaskan gold fields. I've often wondered why Nathan never returned to marry Aunt Marnie." Kimberly wrapped her arms around her knees, looking cuddly in her jeans and fuzzy white sweater. She shook her head and puckered her mouth in a thoughtful expression. " I guess I've always felt a strange desire to come here, even when I was a little girl. Marnie and Nathan's history is such a tragic love story, like a fairytale. My family's 'don't talk about it' attitude just increased my fascination." She smiled. "I used to pretend that I was Marnie and I'd try to imagine a happy ending for them." Her smile faded. "I never could, though. Happy day dreams can't change sad reality." She sighed. "I wonder if Nathan was ever in this area."

Something in her mood disturbed David. He swung his legs over the edge of the bed and stooped to pick up Kimberly's shoes and socks. "Let's get some lunch. I've got a surprise planned for you this afternoon, and we can't be late." He handed her a sock, and pulled one of her feet into his lap. "You probably won't have to do a lot of walking this time," he said, slipping her toes into the other sock. Pausing for a moment, his face broke into a grin. He grasped her ankle and began tickling her foot.

"Stop it, David," she yelled, kicking at his arm as she fell back onto the bed, writhing and laughing. Suddenly twisting to the side, she jerked her foot free. The momentum reeled her off the edge of the bed, and she landed on the floor with a thud.

"Oh Honey, I'm sorry," David said, laying across the bed and leaning over her. "Are you hurt?"

Suddenly, Kimberly's arms encircled David's upper body and she pulled hard. Already off balance, he slid from the bed falling beside her onto the floor. Before he could react, she pounced on him sitting on his belly and bouncing.

"Don't!" he laughed as he gasped for air. Then he lifted her off him and rolled her to the side, resuming his playful attack by tickling her tummy as she kicked and squealed. Finally, they both lay on the floor laughing and short of breath.

Kimberly lifted herself up on one elbow. "You said you were in a hurry. Just what is this big surprise you have planned? I thought we were going to take in more of the sights and attend some of the shows."

"We'll do that tonight. This is something special just for you," David said, pulling Kimberly into his arms.

Lying together on the hand woven rug covering the wooden floor of the old hotel room, Kimberly and David embraced and their kiss was warm. "I love you, David," she whispered.

"I love you back," he answered. Then feeling her closeness against him, smelling the perfume of her soft hair as it fell against his face, all sense of time was lost in the sweetness of her arms.

Chapter 26

"Hurry Kim," David called as he ran up the path and through the door of the log cabin that served as the heliport office. "Two for the Chilkoot Trail and Glacier Tour please," he said, slapping his traveler's checkbook on the counter.

Kimberly arrived, gasping for breath as David gave the sizes for the glacier boots they would be issued for the tour. He put his arm around her shoulder. "That was close. We barely made it."

"Well, if you weren't such an incurable romantic, we wouldn't have been late," she panted, still trying to catch her breath.

After a short briefing session, the passengers slipped on their boots and followed the pilot to the helicopter pad. David ran a few steps ahead, speaking to the pilot who smiled and nodded. The pilot showed David and an elderly couple through the wide door of the six-seat helicopter, then directed Kimberly to the left front seat opposite his own.

Kimberly looked back at David and the empty seat beside him, her eyes asking an unspoken question. David grinned and nodded. He hadn't meant this to be just a sightseeing tour. It was to be her first lesson.

The pilot welcomed his passengers, demonstrated the use of their headphones, and gave them additional safety instructions. Then he pushed the starter button on the throttle beside him. "Please fasten your seat belts and enjoy your tour," he said. Turning his attention to Kimberly, he explained the starting procedure.

The winding up of the engine increased in volume as the pilot gradually advanced the throttle. The sound inside the helicopter was surprisingly quiet though. Only a slight shudder passed through the cabin while the huge propeller blade spun faster and faster, flattening the grass around the platform.

The pilot moved his hand from the throttle to a lever on the console between him and Kimberly.

"What's that for?" Kimberly asked, pressing the communication button on the cord of her headset.

"This is the collective," he answered. "It puts pitch in the blades so the helicopter can lift off or descend." He pulled up on the collective, then he gently moved another lever sticking up from the floor in front of him. The helicopter lifted from the ground, moving into the clear blue sky.

"I'm amazed. I didn't feel us take off," Kimberly said. "I thought it would be more like an express elevator. It's so smooth though, kind of like riding a magic carpet."

The pilot nodded his acknowledgment, then spoke into his headset. "Ladies and Gentlemen, your tour today should be pleasant and relatively warm. The weather is favorable, and there's very little wind, not always the case at Skagway, an Indian name meaning, "Home of the North Wind."

"What does that stick in front of you do?" Kimberly asked, oblivious to colorful Indian names and north winds.

"It's called the cyclic," he answered. "It controls the movement and direction of the chopper."

"How fast are we going?" Kimberly asked.

"We're traveling at a hundred and twenty knots."

"How fast is that in miles per hour?"

"About one hundred thirty-eight miles per hour." He spoke again to his passengers. "Below you is the Taiya inlet, passageway for about twenty thousand men who came through Skagway on route to prospect for that shiny yellow stuff that drove men crazy. A condition known as gold fever. The gold rush in the area you'll see today only lasted from 1898 to 1900, but thousands of hungry men poured in trying to satisfy their appetites. Some succeeded, but most left the gold fields exhausted and beaten, sadder, wiser, and still hungry."

"How long did it take to complete your flight training?" Kimberly broke into his narration like a thoughtless child.

"About a year, ma'am."

"Was it hard to get accepted?" she asked, her eyes glued to

the mass of instruments on the control panel. "How much does the training cost?"

The pilot glanced back at his passengers with a helpless shrug. David did too, wearing a sheepish grin on his beet-red face. He was relieved to see the gray-haired people smiling and nodding their understanding.

The pilot patiently answered Kimberly's questions until she finally grew quiet, gazing out the window for the first time since she'd gotten on board.

The pilot studied her for a moment, expecting more questions. He winked at David, then proceeded with his customary narration. "Below us is the tiny settlement of Dyea. In 1898, about ten thousand people resided in this second jumping-off point for the treacherous six-hundred-mile journey to the Klondike gold fields in the Yukon Territory of Canada. During the gold rush, many prospectors strained beyond endurance only to clasp a few gold nuggets in their callused hands. A lot of them died at the hands of ruthless claim jumpers. Many others became victims of the merciless weather and wild country which was, and still can be, deadly; especially for those who are unfamiliar with this final great frontier.

"We will view portions of the famous Chilkoot Trail, including the remarkable "golden stairs," a torturous forty-degree climb on shale or ice that prospectors had to take to reach the Chilkoot Pass and the border of British Columbia. From there, they began the downhill trek to the Yukon River. The gold seekers then traveled five hundred miles up the Yukon to the gold fields."

Kimberly looked at the vast landscape below, watching a group of mountain goats grazing on a mountainside. Soon the helicopter hovered above the Chilkoot Trail. The famous trail, still clearly visible, stretched up the steep slope to the summit. Suddenly, a haunting loneliness gathered around Kimberly. She looked at the rugged shale pathway, sensing an odd kinship with the heart-bursting strain of those who had struggled there all for the sake of a dream. The melancholy lingered, pressing on her mind.

Sensing Kimberly's mood, David frowned as he recalled her distraction earlier that day in the hotel room. Now she again seemed far away.

As the helicopter moved beyond the gold fields. Kimberly's attention returned to the cockpit.

The pilot cheerfully juggled his narration between the great state of Alaska and technical information. Kimberly was like a sponge as he explained the control panel's artificial horizon, altitude indicators, compass, radio and instruments.

Gradually the entire face of the untamed wilderness changed, and the helicopter hovered above the spectacular Valley of the Glaciers. The blue-white ice fields like ancient giants of a forgotten era seemed to flow like rivers between high mountain peaks. The pilot maneuvered the collective lever, settling the helicopter on one of the glaciers, and rolled back the throttle to a ground idle. A tour guide who helped them exit the cabin greeted the passengers.

Peering through crystal blue ice beneath their feet, David and Kimberly tested the slipperiness of the surface and found their footing secure under the rubber soles of their boots. Then they were led back through endless time into the cold rugged majesty of the polar ice age.

Chapter 27

The following morning, David rented a small four-wheel-drive van and loaded their luggage into the back of the vehicle. After a "prospector's breakfast," he and Kimberly left Skagway and drove up the beautiful Klondike Highway toward Carcross, a small Indian settlement along one of Alaska's most scenic byways.

The Skagway River foamed and boiled over rocks and boulders, plunging through White Pass Canyon beside the highway. Awestruck by the lush greenery of the steep canyon walls and the rampaging river, David was distracted. Kimberly became nervous as he had to swerve back into his lane several times after losing his focus on the road to peer out the windows. Around a bend, he suddenly saw an old tourist train steaming through the canyon on the opposite side of the river.

"Wow! Look at that," he said, nearly running off the road.

"David, pull over. You look. I'll drive," Kimberly ordered. "I don't fancy the idea of tumbling back to Skagway through the rapids."

"Okay," he said with a silly grin as he pulled to the side of the road. He had barely brought the van to a halt when he grabbed his camera from the glove box, leaped out of the car, and nearly walked in front of a pickup truck as it sped past. He jumped back at the sound of the horn, then hurried across the highway and lifted his camera to focus on the puffing steam engine.

Kimberly, a little shaken by his careless distraction, laid her head against the back of the seat and sighed deeply. She had never seen this excitable reckless side of David. Then she recalled a stormy night on Thunder Mountain and a near-fatal accident involving this city greenhorn and his horse. Well, maybe she had seen a careless streak after all and just hadn't realized it. She slid into the driver's seat, watching David's intense creative genius as he saw painting after painting through the glass eye of his camera. He took a few steps forward, backed up several feet, then moved forward again. He was peering through the camera when he walked smack into the guardrail.

Kimberly giggled.

David stared at the guardrail like it had appeared from nowhere. Then he climbed onto it, balancing above the river to snap several more pictures of the train as it lumbered along the canyon wall.

Kimberly gripped the steering wheel holding her breath until David stepped down from his precarious perch. He was beaming like a little boy on Christmas morning when he returned to the van.

"David, don't do stupid things like that," she scolded, pulling back onto the highway.

"Like what?" He grinned, but became serious when he saw she was truly worried. "Hey Kim, I was okay. I didn't mean to worry you," he said, putting his hand on her knee.

"Worry me! I was terrified. That dumb train wasn't that important. I stood by you once while your life hung by a thread. I don't want to ever go through that again." Kimberly swallowed hard. "You take too many chances," she growled, focusing on the road ahead.

"I'm sorry, honey," David said, kneeling between the seats and slipping his arm around her shoulder. "Getting off the trail and tumbling down that glacier yesterday was just an accident. But I guess I have been a little foolhardy today. I promise I'll be more careful."

Kimberly glanced into his repentant eyes, feeling her anger melting away like a sun-drenched icicle. "Thank you," she said.

After at least a dozen more photo stops before reaching the Canadian border, only twenty-two miles from Skagway, Kimberly sat impatiently drumming her fingers on the steering wheel. "He said, 'Stop right here. This is the *perfect* spot to photograph that moose,' that is a hundred miles out in the marsh," she complained to herself. "So I stop right here in this *perfect* spot, and he walks halfway across the meadow to take the picture. If he doesn't step in black muck and disappear forever, he'll probably get trampled by a mad moose, and I'll still be a twenty-two-year-old widow."

Finally David returned wearing his Christmas grin. His feet were sloshing, and his wet jeans clung to his boot tops.

"The perfect spot, huh?" Kimberly taunted as he climbed into the van. "David, the tourist information said not to get off the trails and roads. The ground can be very unstable."

"I know, but I was being careful."

"Sure you were. Anyway, at this rate we'll never make it to Whitehorse tonight."

"So we'll stay at the motel in Carcross or at a cabin on Spirit Lake. Relax, Kim. This is our honeymoon."

"Maybe you ought to take your camera and go honeymoon a bear." The twinkle in her eyes took the slight sharpness off the edge of her voice as she steered onto the highway again.

"Okay, no more pictures until Carcross," he vowed.

They crossed into Canada and continued to the border checkpoint. While Kimberly freshened up in the restroom, David gathered information and cleared the van and their identification for entry into Canada's Yukon Territory.

"Kim, I know I promised no more pictures," he pleaded when she returned, "but do you think you could endure one more session? The guy said we'd be driving past some outstanding ice fields soon. Anyway, think of the money my paintings from these shots will bring. You know, savings for your helicopter."

Kimberly frowned at him for a moment, then broke into a smile. "Of course I can, David. I'm really not a tyrant. I want you to enjoy yourself. It's just that you climb mountains, ford rivers, and risk the very jaws of death for your pictures. I appreciate your talent, Honey, but you do get carried away sometimes. Besides, if you photograph every unique or beautiful part of Alaska, I'll be too old to take flight training when we finally do get back home."

"You're right. Kim . . . compromise?" David asked, stretching out his hand.

"Sure," she answered, slipping her hand into his. He pulled her to him, warming her to her toes with a disarming kiss.

Late that night, David and Kimberly strolled hand in hand along the tree lined shore of Spirit Lake. Except for the stream of light glowing from their window and the gray shadow of their cabin against the spruce trees, there was no other visible sign of man. Several faint stars appeared in the darker edge of the pale gray sky. Stillness surrounded them, disturbed only by an occasional call of a night bird or the gruff echo of a bullfrog. It seemed as though humanity had ceased to exist and they were alone in a wild mysterious land. The beautiful haunting cry of a wolf stirred the silence, hanging in the cool August night air like the final strains of a dying symphony.

Kimberly shivered and pulled her jacket more tightly about her as a breeze drifted across the lake, rippling the water against the shore. "It's so wonderfully primitive here," she whispered, trying not to disturb the sacred quiet of this untouched place.

David encircled her waist with his arms, resting his chin on her head. "Yes it is," he whispered, sensing the same reverence. Suddenly he felt Kimberly's body stiffen.

"Someone else is here." She spoke so faintly, David could barely hear, but her words sent a sudden chill through him.

She pulled away. Moving toward the lake, she stood as though she were spellbound on the shore. "Kim, what's wrong," David asked, while icy prickles crawled beneath his skin. She didn't respond. Unnerved by her frozen trance, he rushed forward, placing his hands on her shoulders and spun her about. "Kimberly, what is it?"

In the deep shadows cast by the Northland's midnight sun, he saw her face, pale and transfixed. Then her eyelids fluttered, and she crumpled in his arms.

"Kimberly," he cried. Confusion and fear tore through him as he lifted her and ran stumbling through the twilight toward the cabin.

David paced anxiously beside the bed, watching Kimberly. He cursed himself for not taking her suggestion to sign up for an Alaskan tour rather than traveling on their own. He suddenly resented the vast isolation surrounding them. Condemning himself for not hurrying on to Whitehorse, he battled feelings of helplessness and fear. He wanted to rush her to a hospital, to put her in the skilled hands of a physician who could bring her back. Yet deep inside, truth forced its way through his denial, and he knew whatever had happened to her was not physical.

Recalling vivid dreams of Marnie and the ominous presence of the unknown made David's skin turn cold. *Spirit Lake,* he thought. *How ironic. Probably named by some superstitious Indian.* He denounced the spirits in his mind and sat on the bed beside his wife. He gathered her in his arms, rocking her back and forth. "Come on Kim, please Honey, you've got to wake up." Burying his face in her hair, he whispered a prayer.

"What's wrong, David?"

The sound of Kimberly's voice in the hushed room startled him. He jumped, taking a quick breath. "Kim? Oh Kimmy, are you okay?"

She nodded, but her eyes looked confused and glassy.

David held her tightly, controlling the trembling which was replacing the tenseness in his body. "Honey, what happened out there? You scared the daylights out of me."

"I don't know. I was standing by the lake. Suddenly I felt awfully weak. Then I don't remember anything. How did we get in here?"

"You fainted. You said something about someone else being there. Then you just fainted."

"Someone else was there," she sat up. "He spoke to me. His voice was clear, but I couldn't understand the language. He touched me and said, "Basi sechoya, no'ideyo." The words are imprinted on my mind, but I don't know what they mean."

David shuddered. "Do you feel well enough to travel? This place is giving me the creeps. I think we need to get away from here."

"Right now?" Kimberly asked, looking at her husband with a dazed far away expression. "David, I'm exhausted, and I have a terrible headache. Can't we just get a good night's sleep?"

"Kim, I don't know what this is all about, but I can't sleep here now."

"It'll be okay, David." Kimberly snuggled into the covers and pulled them up to her chin, closing her eyes as she laid her head on the pillow. "I don't know who touched me, but the touch was . . . warm." Within seconds she was asleep.

David hesitated, trying to justify his desire to drag her out of a comfortable bed and whisk her away in the night. It wasn't like there was another motel just down the road. Finally he shrugged, pulled off his boots, and crawled in beside her, but even fitful sleep seemed as far away as home.

Chapter 28

The beautiful Canadian landscape rolled by unnoticed as David and Kimberly sped along the highway. Kimberly stared blankly out of the side window. David's jaw was set, his grip fierce on the steering wheel. His eyes darted between the road and troubled glances at Kimberly while miles swept by in silence.

As they passed a road sign identifying the Alaskan Highway, Kimberly looked puzzled. "I thought we were on the Klondike Highway heading toward Dawson and the gold rush area," she said.

David shook his head. "No, I took the highway to Fairbanks at the junction out of Whitehorse. I want to get to a city where there's some help if we need it."

"David, I told you I'm fine. There's no reason to change our original plans. I'm just a little tired today, that's all."

"Yes, I know that's what you said, but you hardly muttered a sound at breakfast, and you haven't spoken more than five words in the last hundred and fifty miles. Yet, I don't see you sleeping, either." He glanced at her, and she was taken aback by the worried furrow on his brow and the determined fire in his eyes. "I'm sorry if it sounds like I'm doubting your word, Kim, but the symptoms just don't fit the claims. I have no idea what happened last night, but I know it did have a dramatic effect on you. Whether this thing is physical, emotional, or just plain weird, I have to follow my feelings. I'm not going to be helpless in the middle of nowhere like I was last night. I'd really like to just fly us home tonight, but before we do anything, I'm taking you to a doctor for my own piece of mind."

"David, I don't want to go home. I am all right. I apologize if I've been a little preoccupied."

"A little preoccupied?" David cut in. "Kim, you've been like a stranger ever since you fainted last night. What am I supposed to do? Just go on pretending we're floating on some fluffy cloud toward happily ever after? Oh sure, my wife hears voices I can't hear, collapses in my arms for no apparent reason, then stares at nothing all day like a dumb block of ice, and she's fine? Kimberly, I've met the unknown before, and I didn't much like the experience."

Kimberly bristled as a flush of pink tinted her cheeks. "A dumb block of ice? That's very complimentary, David." She folded her arms across her chest and pouted.

"Honey, I didn't mean it that way. I guess I'm tired and cranky." He rubbed the taut muscles in his neck. "After some ghost in the wind ripped you from me last night, I never shut my eyes, and today has brought no peace. Your mood comes way short of any reassurance." His eyes softened, speaking concern and love more deeply than words could express.

"I'm sorry David," she said, relaxing her arms and taking his hand in hers. She squeezed his fingers. "Let's go on to Fairbanks. I'll see a doctor, then if he says I'm okay, we can take up where we left off and enjoy the rest of our honeymoon. I still want to go to Denali and Anchorage and all the places we planned." Her smile was warm and sincere, but her eyes didn't smile. "Maybe cutting out the Klondike is wise, all things considered. We can relax and unwind closer to civilization." She kissed his hand. "In the meantime, slow down and enjoy the drive. Take some pictures. I really am fine. Okay?"

David's expression was skeptical. Finally, he nodded. "Okay, but the doctor is an absolute."

As they drove along the timber lined highway, Kimberly pointed toward a meadow through a break in the trees. "David, look! There's a bear!"

David brought the van to a rapid halt alongside the highway. "Wow, he's big . . . must be a grizzly. The only wild bear I've ever seen before was a cub Jerry had a fight with over some fish. This one's magnificent." David opened the car door and reached for his camera.

"David, don't you dare go out there to get a picture," Kimberly said, catching his arm.

"I won't, I won't. I'm not an idiot," he said, pulling loose from her grasp. "I'm just going to stand in the door and get a shot over the roof."

"You mean there is hope that we might actually leave Alaska with you still in one piece? What happened to the absolute need to photograph from the perfect spot?" she teased.

"This is a perfect spot," David said, elevating himself by stepping on the seat. Seconds later, he pulled himself onto the van roof with one leg dangling in the open doorway. Gradually his dangling leg moved along the front of the windshield, then finally hung over Kimberly's side window.

"How did I know he wouldn't be satisfied standing in the door?" Kimberly mumbled, shaking her head.

Lumbering across the meadow, the bear noticed the stopped vehicle and halted, turning to study David.

"David, get back in here. He's looking at us," Kimberly said.

"Be quiet, you'll scare him away."

"If I'm the one scaring him, why is my heart pounding so hard? Come on David, this is no cub. Now get back in here!"

The bear rose on its hind legs, towering like a brown giant. It tossed its enormous head back and forth, thrashing the air with its paw while a deep throaty growl rolled from its mouth.

"David please," Kimberly pleaded. "I had a run-in with a bear once, and it nearly cost me my life." The bear took several threatening lunges toward the van. "David—" Kimberly cried. Her voice broke, then went hoarse as the last part of his name stuck in her vocal cords. She quickly rolled up her window. David slowly slid back across the roof and stood on the seat, still snapping pictures as Kimberly tugged on his pant legs. "David, let's get out of here now," she squeaked.

David took one last picture, then slid into his seat and slammed the door as the bear dropped to all four feet and charged toward the van. Quickly accelerating away from the roadside, David glanced in his rearview mirror. The animal rose again on hind feet, tossing its huge head and warning the intruders that this wild land belonged to the bears.

David turned his head toward Kimberly and winced, feeling her glare boring through him. "I was being careful, Kimmy. I never even left the car."

She shook her head, then laid it against the back of the seat. "And I worry him," she mumbled to herself.

"What?" he asked.

"Nothing, dear, I was talking to the bear."

David and Kimberly buried their noses in the map, adopting a new agenda while lunching at Haines Junction. To their left along the Alaskan Highway lay the spectacular beauty of Canada's Kluane National Park. Still trying to put David's mind at ease, Kimberly repeatedly assured him that she was fine. Kimberly pressed David to take advantage of the sights while they were there, finally convincing him they could stay the night in Tok, then proceed to Fairbanks the following day.

They spent the rest of the afternoon and evening walking hand in hand along the park trails. As they embraced beside the clear blue waters of Kluane Lake, the events of the night before were forgotten in the sweet depths of their kiss. Cuddling in each other's arms, they stared spellbound at Kaskawulsh Glacier: three massive ice-blue rivers flowing through the rugged St. Elias Mountains. Later, as they strolled below the thundering waters of Donjek Falls, their expressions of love were lost to anyone but themselves. The honeymoon had begun again.

That night, David fell into bed while Kimberly showered, applied light make-up, and dressed in her favorite sky blue nightgown. Its delicate folds swished softly against her legs as she moved to the bed and lay down, snuggling against her husband. A loud snore erupted from his mouth. He groaned, rolling away from her and snored again.

Kimberly frowned at his back. "Humph, that was all a waste

of time and make-up." Then she smiled and passed her hand across his back. Oh well, what did I expect after he stayed up all night worrying about me? She ran her fingers through the short hair at the base of his neck. "I'm sorry, Honey," she whispered.

She sighed and leaned against the headboard. Her smile faded as the memory of her strange experience at Spirit Lake filled the room. I don't understand what happened, she thought. Who was standing beside me? She wrapped her arms around her knees, hugging them against her chest. I felt a presence so strongly. "Basi sechoya, no'ideyo," she mumbled, staring into the darkness. "What does it mean? Who touched me?"

Chapter 29

The next day Kimberly and David reached Fairbanks, Alaska. Kimberly couldn't explain a thrill passing through her as David drove into the heart of the city. She felt an odd sense of elation, almost like she was coming home after years of being away. *How strange . . . I've never been here,* she thought. *In fact, a lot of things are more than strange. Is it just because I always wanted to visit Alaska? Why, for that matter, have I always wanted to visit Alaska? Why was I so excited when David said he wanted to come here for our honeymoon? It's something more to me than the primitive beauty or even curiosity about Nathan . . . but what? I've felt . . . almost home-sick since we arrived in Skagway, yet the homesickness isn't for home.* She sighed, gazing at the Chena River that flowed alongside the road.

They passed a sod-roofed log cabin that served as a visitor's center and David said, "Well that was easy. We won't have far to go for a source of tourist information. That's our hotel just down the street. After we secure our reservations and get an appointment with a doctor, we'll come back and see what Fairbanks has to offer."

"See, I told you there's nothing wrong with me," Kimberly said as she and David left the doctor's office. "Now, will you please stop worrying so we can relax and enjoy our honeymoon?"

With only a hint of relief in his eyes, David stopped and looked at Kimberly. "That depends a lot on you, Kim. A clean bill of health still doesn't explain much." He put his arm around her shoulder and walked her to the car.

Fairbanks was founded by E.T. Barnette, a turn of the century entrepreneur at the start of the Fairbanks district gold rush in 1902. The city contained many historical houses and buildings. It was alive with frontier history. Yet it also carried a modern progressive air.

During the next few days, David and Kimberly visited museums, and took walking and driving tours. They admired unique Alaskan art, which blended themes of native heritage, history, wildlife, and rugged wilderness with contemporary themes.

The newlyweds took a ride on a restored narrow gauge rail to a gold camp and panned for gold. At the University of Alaska Arctic Biology Research Center, they saw caribou, reindeer, moose, and the one time nearly extinct musk oxen.

One afternoon, they relaxed on a stern-wheeler cruise down the Chena and Tanana rivers. Then they drove to the North Pole fifteen miles from Fairbanks and relived childhood in the fantasy store that could only belong to Santa Claus.

"It's a good thing we didn't go to Dawson," Kimberly said as she fell into bed that night. "I wanted to visit an old mining town, but how could we have fit it in?"

"How about a drive up the Steese highway tomorrow?" Daivd suggested. "Central is only about a hundred miles away and it's an old mining town. Then we can soak in a hot-springs until we turn into prunes before we come back to Fairbanks."

"Sounds divine," Kimberly answered as she snuggled in the comfort of David's arms.

They expected a ghost town, so David and Kimberly were surprised to find that the old mining community of Central was inhabited, and the area was still being mined. Most of the town structures were small, built of logs and wood planks, and battered by age and harsh weather.

David was drawn to the antique setting, snapping picture

after picture. However, Kimberly seemed oddly intrigued by early mining operations and history, hardly noticing the surroundings. She asked dozens of questions whenever she could trap an informant.

"What's with you, Kim?" David asked during a brief moment when he caught her attention. "Remember me? I'm your husband. That's the third time you've just walked away with any old sourdough who'd talk to you. Since when did you become so taken with mining?"

Kimberly looked at David, considering his question. "I don't know," she said, shrugging with an uncertain expression on her face. "I guess I wanted some answers."

"Answers to what?'

"Uh . . . nothing important, just curious. I'm sorry." She hooked her arm through David's.

Puzzled at her behavior, he shook his head. "Let's drive to the resort and take a dip in the pool. My feet are tired."

David secured a room in the three-story hotel at the hot springs. Nestled at the foot of a mountain among birch, poplar, aspen, and scattered spruce, the hotel's Victorian atmosphere was romantic and inviting.

Playing in the modern swimming pool fed by the hot springs, David and Kimberly splashed and dunked each other. Then they swam for awhile. Finally, when their energy was spent, they relaxed together in the warm water. As they cuddled in the far corner, their lips met again and again. Soon the world was forgotten. They retired to their room as their closeness stirred the sweet intimacy that belonged to them as husband and wife.

Chapter 30

Following a delicious home-cooked breakfast at the hot springs lodge, David and Kimberly enjoyed another leisurely swim in the pool. Then they showered and dressed and drove back on the gravel highway to Fairbanks.

They ate lunch in Fairbanks, then took the Parks Highway toward Anchorage. A strange emptiness came over Kimberly as the city faded in the distance. "I feel like we've forgotten something, David. Are you sure you packed everything?'

"Yes, I did. You didn't leave your purse at the restaurant did you?" he asked.

"No, it's right here by my feet."

"We didn't forget anything then."

Kimberly looked out the side window and frowned. Eventually her eyelids grew heavy. She settled back in the seat and drifted off to sleep.

David cast a troubled glance at his wife. Ever since they left the hot springs, she had again seemed unusually quiet and distracted. The distant look in her eyes was back.

David began to wonder if Kimberly might have a history of moodiness or depression.

Two hours later, he secured their reservations at a cedar lodge in Denali State Park bordering Mt. McKinley National Park. Their room was spacious and had a fine view overlooking the wild mountain-born Nenana River.

"What a beautiful place to stay," Kimberly said, giving David a hug. "It's absolutely perfect." Kimberly's smile and excitement didn't seem quite natural, but she was clearly trying to be herself, and David felt encouraged.

Through the late afternoon and evening, they took photographs of brilliant lupine and fireweed growing in swaths and patches in mountain glades and on the tundra. They hiked on park trails and sat near the riverbank watching small wildlife, and even a mother moose and her baby came to drink.

Early the next morning, they boarded a shuttle bus for an eighty-nine mile tour through the spectacular, six-million-acre wilderness and wildlife preserve of Mt. McKinley National Park. As the bus lumbered through the park, David pointed out the bus window. "Look, there it is!"

Mt McKinley rose through the clouds to an awesome height above the tundra in breathtaking grandeur. The mountain, renamed by politicians, loomed rugged and forbidding in the distance. Magnified even larger by the dense cold of the high altitude, its icy slopes appeared pink in the slanted sun. The huge massif proclaimed its original and more revered Indian name, Denali: "The Great One."

"How magnificent," Kimberly said, gazing out the window. "The tallest mountain in North America."

David was silent, painting scene after scene in his mind. Suddenly, he remembered his camera and began snapping pictures.

David woke up before five the next morning and found Kimberly's side of the bed empty. He turned over and saw her standing in front of the window, her slender form silhouetted by the dim light. He got up and slipped his arms around her waist, drawing her close. "Couldn't you sleep?" he asked. Kimberly shook her head but said nothing.

David glanced out the window. Although full darkness didn't fall during the summer upon this northern land, the surrounding mountains held the valley in shadows. The morning sky was overcast. "Clouds covering the mountains today," he said. "I hope it doesn't rain out our float trip down the river."

"We have to go back." Kimberly's voice was a whisper.

"What?" David asked.

"We have to go back to Fairbanks."

"Fairbanks! Why?"

"We have to go back today."

"Whatever for? Did you forget something after all?"

Kimberly shook her head. David was baffled. "Then why?" he pressed.

"I-I don't know."

"Kimberly, this doesn't make any sense! We're more than a third of the way to Anchorage. You've got to at least have a reason."

She turned to face David. "I don't . . . I just . . ."

David was startled to see a tear trailing down her cheek. She hung her head. "I don't know why. Please, we just have to."

David paced across the room and threw his hands in the air. He turned around, opening his mouth to argue, but Kimberly's slumped shoulders and pained face held him in check. Finally, he walked over and took her in his arms. "Okay Honey," he said, looking at the gloomy horizon as his eyes clouded with worry. "If you feel that strongly about it, we'll go back. Maybe we can just fly home from there."

The only sounds in the van were the rhythm of the windshield wipers and the raindrops pelting the van roof. Several times during the hundred-and-twenty-mile drive to Fairbanks, David tried to pry some sense out of Kimberly, but she seemed as confused as he was.

Most of the trip passed in silence, and David formed a plan to get Kimberly to see a psychiatrist. Maybe hypnosis or some medication would bring things out in the open. Something was happening in her head, and David needed some answers.

Kimberly felt miserable. She knew she was wrecking their honeymoon and she didn't even know why. When they were in Central, she had felt a strong impression that she needed some information about mining. Then after having lunch in Fairbanks, she had pushed away a nagging feeling that they shouldn't leave. This morning she had been awakened by an unspoken message so powerful that she could not suppress what she now recognized as a premonition. *There's something in Fairbanks I have to do*, she thought, wringing her hands. *And I don't even know what it is. David's trying so hard to stay calm. He must have a million questions, and I don't even have one answer. Maybe if I just satisfy one question, I'll finally find some peace.*

They reached Fairbanks and Kimberly asked to stop at the visitor's center. When she ran inside, David grabbed the chance to find a phone and set up an appointment with a doctor. A short time later, Kimberly hurried toward the van and opened the door. She was pale and out of breath. "Take me to this address, David," she ordered. Suddenly feeling weak and dizzy, she grasped the door handle to keep from falling.

David jumped out of the van and ran around it, catching her in his arms. "I'm taking you nowhere but to a doctor."

Kimberly caught her balance and pushed him away. "No, I don't need a doctor. Please just do as I ask."

"Kimberly, I'm not messing around with this anymore. I'll do what I think is best," David insisted, grabbing her wrists.

"Leave me alone!" she yelled, pulling her arms free. "I'll take myself there if you won't." She ran through the rain toward a bronze statue in the park that adjoined the visitor's center. Suddenly, she came to her senses and started to cry, slumping down on the wet rocks surrounding the statue.

Stunned and worried, David stood beside the van as a cold raindrop slipped beneath his jacket and trickled down his back. He pulled his collar higher, then slowly walked to the statue and sat on the wall beside his wife. "What's happening to us, Kim? I love you, but . . . I don't even know you anymore. I don't know what went wrong." Swallowing a lump in his throat, he mumbled, "I wish we'd never come to Alaska." He stared at the red bricks beneath his feet, listening to Kimberly sniffling. Then he gently slipped his arm around her shoulders.

She leaned against him, blending tears with the rain on his jacket. "I'm sorry, David. I didn't mean to yell at you. I've been so confused because things keep happening. Feelings that I'm not doing something I have to do. I didn't want to come back. I hated to ask you to bring me back. I wanted our honeymoon to be so perfect . . . but there's something here in Fairbanks I must find out. Please try to understand."

"I am trying to understand, Kim. But you keep scaring me. You almost fainted again back there and your face was as white as a ghost."

She sat up and wiped her nose with the back of her hand. "I'm all right David. I think I just hyperventilated and got a little dizzy." He reached into his back pocket and handed her a handkerchief. She dabbed at her tears and blew her nose. "It's just been upsetting to have all these feelings and not know what they mean."

There was a familiar echo in her words. David's heart softened as he recalled his argument with Jerry at Indian Lake last May.

Kimberly stood up, gazing at the bronze statue, the figures of the unknown first pioneer family in Fairbanks. "Family," she said as the fleeting hint of a revelation crossed her mind. "Something about family." She sighed and sat back down. "Whatever it is . . . everything that has happened, including that night at Spirit Lake . . . it's like someone has been pulling me here. The answers are close, David. I can feel it."

"Okay," David whispered, kissing her forehead. "Where did you want me to take you?" He reached for the crumpled address in her hand.

"It's the district recorder's office. I'll just ask them a few questions and . . ." Kimberly gave a sudden gasp. Her heart began pounding as warm tingles passed through her. Looking down, she rubbed the goosebumps that were breaking out on her arms. "David, that's what I'm supposed to do! I have no idea why, but I-I think I'm supposed to search for Nathan's claim," she stammered.

"What? Kimberly, this is our honeymoon."

"I know. It's ridiculous and probably impossible after all these years anyway. I'm sorry, David. I don't want to make a worse mess of our honeymoon than I already have, but . . ."

David's stunned gaze bored through her. She hung her head, looking pitiful. David stood up, making a hopeless gesture with his arms and walked a short distance away. He stopped, his eyes focused on the ground as he relinquished his own desires, willing himself to follow hidden ghosts from the past. The memory of his dreams, Marnie's outstretched hand and grief-stricken face returned like a vision to his mind. He knew her love for Kimberly reached beyond the bands of death, but there had always been something more to the dreams. An unspoken message he had yet to understand. Maybe this was what Marnie had been trying to tell him.

David walked back and placed his hand on Kimberly's shoulder. "Well Honey, one thing is certain. Ignoring this persistent urge of yours isn't getting us anywhere."

Shaking his head, he reached for her hand. "Come on, let's go find your great-aunt's missing boyfriend's claim."

Chapter 31

"Ma'am, you need to realize that even if I do find his claim on file, there's no guarantee we can pinpoint the actual location," the recording clerk said as he scanned the view screen of his microfiche. "What was his full name again?"

"Nathan Demeron," Kimberly said, nervously rocking on her heels.

A young man with black hair and black eyes who had followed David and Kimberly into the office glanced up from a magazine he was browsing through. His slender features and high cheekbones were Indian, but his olive skin was lighter than most Native Americans.

"The problem with these old claims is figuring out the legal descriptions," the clerk said. "Without any law and order in those days, there was a lot of claim jumping. Most miners filed using sly or clever legal descriptions that kept others from finding their claims." He paused, reading the microfiche. "Well, you're in luck. He did mine in this region and filed a claim at the recorder's headquarters in Circle in 1903. All those old records have been transferred here now."

Kimberly's heart jumped as goosebumps again prickled her arms and a thrill passed through her. She squeezed David's hand eagerly leaning forward to see the screen.

The clerk mumbled, reading to himself. "Hmmm . . . two days by canoe from the Tolovana River to Hope Creek. Four more days up the creek toward Smoking Mountain above the beaver dam where the great tree leaps to the sky."

"That's it?" David asked.

"Afraid so," the clerk answered. "Not much to go on."

"Where's Hope Creek?" Kimberly asked. "At least that would give us a starting place."

"Who knows? I can try to find it on a map if you can come

back later, but most of these creeks were named by miners. The names were seldom recorded on maps back then. It'll be like looking for a nugget in a wilderness, but I'll try."

Kimberly's shoulders slumped. "Thank you," she mumbled, turning away.

David smiled and shook the clerk's hand. "Thanks, we'll get a hotel room and come back after lunch."

As David held the door for Kimberly, the clerk nodded at the young Indian. "Mr. Duncan? What can I help you with?"

"Can I switch my appointment to this afternoon?" the young man asked. "Something has come up."

"Sure, come in right at one. I'll help you before I get tied down with that other couple. Their research will take a while."

David was just about to close Kimberly's door when the Indian approached their van. "I'm sorry to bother you," he said, "but I couldn't help overhearing your conversation. I know it's none of my business, but could you tell me why you want to locate this old claim?"

"Personal reasons," David said, eyeing him skeptically, but Kimberly's interest was aroused.

"Nathan Demeron, the man who owned the claim, was going to marry one of my relatives, but he disappeared shortly after he found gold here. We'd like to find out what happened to him," she volunteered.

"I'm Eric Duncan," the man said, extending his hand to David and Kimberly. "I may be able to help you if you can also be of assistance to me. Could we discuss it over lunch?" David hesitated, studying Eric with an air of suspicion, but Kimberly readily agreed.

Eric's dark eyes examined David and Kimberly as they sat at a booth waiting for their orders. David watched him back, wondering why he was so quiet after being so direct. Where were the usual questions: Where are you from? How long are you staying?

Finally Eric spoke. "You know, there's not much wealth to be gained in a gold mine, and the grueling work can kill you." He shifted in his seat. "Are you interested in mining?" Eric seemed bold against his own will, out of character, almost like he was really more reserved.

"Not particularly," David answered with an attitude of caution. "Why do you want to know?"

Eric fidgeted with his napkin, but his gaze was unflinching.

Kimberly's curiosity knew no caution. "You said you could help us?" she asked, leaning forward, her eyes searching the black depths of Eric's eyes with eager anticipation.

Eric remained silent, clearly uncertain of his plan. Kimberly and David exchanged nervous glances.

Then a look of determination replaced the uneasiness in Eric's face. He set his napkin on the table and took a drink of water. "I said I could help you because . . ." he sat upright, taking a long, deep breath, "because my father mines the claim you are looking for."

The glass of juice in Kimberly's hand crashed to the table. David and Eric grabbed napkins and began sopping up the spilled juice. Kimberly sat motionless with her mouth open.

Eric went on to explain. "My father is white. My mother was Athabaskan Indian. Before she died, she told my sister and me about the white man her grandfather had befriended. After her grandfather had helped him find gold, he established the claim we work, on what is now called Brooks Creek. Later the man discovered a rich vein of gold in a natural cave somewhere on the claim. My great-grandfather was a strong believer that mining inside the earth was taboo. He warned the white man, but he didn't listen. Then the man vanished, and my great-grandfather never saw him again. The Indians called him Dedezis, but his name was Nathan Demeron."

David pursed his lips to whistle. "Whew, what a coincidence that you just happened to be at the recorder's office when we asked about the claim," David said.

Kimberly sat in reverent awe. "It wasn't coincidence." Her voice was a whisper. "We were supposed to meet. That's why we were brought back today."

"I just flew in from Kodiak this morning." Eric hesitated. "My father's mining claim is in trouble. He was injured during a cave-in of his hard rock mine last winter. Earthquakes are common in the volcanic area of Tolovana Dome, but an unusually strong tremor caused the main audit to collapse.

"I work on a fishing long-liner. My sister Rachel was a nurse in Anchorage. Dad hadn't told us how bad things were, but medical expenses and loss of income forced him to let his help go. He tried placer mining on a creek this summer, but he fell and broke his arm. With all the problems, he failed to meet the annual labor and rental for the claim. Rachel resigned and came home to help him. She found a final notice and called me. I'm here to see if I can get an extension."

Eric sat back as the waitress brought their food. Then he continued. "Father never struck it rich or anything, but he's provided a living and mining is his life. Besides, he knows that rich vein Nathan found is somewhere on the land. If I can arrange the extension, Rachel and I are planning to try to find the cave. Father has hunted for years, but it's got to be there, somewhere. If we can find it, we can save the claim, and Father will be financially secure for the rest of his life. He's getting older and his injuries have taken their toll." Eric made several stabs at an olive with his fork. "Maybe we can help you find some answers." He paused hesitating to ask, then looked up and cleared his throat. "I wondered if maybe you could help us look for the cave."

David and Kimberly were speechless. Finally, David turned to Kimberly. "Well Honey, what do you want to do?"

Kimberly sighed, dissecting a pickle with her fork. "This is so unexpected," she said, glancing at Eric. "You see, we're on our honeymoon. I . . . I've already made a disaster of our plans. I don't know. I feel an urgency to pursue this . . . but it's so unfair to David."

David felt an odd sense of intrigue. He again recalled Marnie's hand reaching out to him, his desire to comfort her sorrow in his dreams. Once she had pleaded for his life. Whatever unknown mystery lay ahead, he owed it to her to see it through.

David put his arm around his wife. "Kim, remember the day

we got married? The taxi broke down, your luggage got lost, and I reserved the wrong cabin on the wrong ferry." He repeated the words he had spoken then. "Honey, since the day we met, our lives have been one crazy adventure." He smiled, lifting her chin and kissing her forehead. "What the heck, we might as well keep going the way we started. Let's follow your feelings and do it."

Chapter 32

In the interest of time, Kimberly insisted they go by helicopter to Eric's father's claim. "Wow, this is an expensive way to save time," David teased as they boarded the chopper. "I know you love to ride in helicopters Kim, but the cost is ridiculous."

Kimberly had no interest in the pilot or inner workings of the helicopter this time. As they flew over the rugged landscape and dense foliage below, her mind was a hundred years away.

Soon, the helicopter landed in a grassy clearing bordered by thick stands of black spruce, birch, and poplar trees. The pilot opened the door for them to exit, and an eager thrill swept through Kimberly. She gripped David's hand and stepped down.

A large cabin made of stripped logs with a high peaked roof stood at the edge of the forest. Nestled deeper beneath the white spruce trees was a small, roughly-hewn log cabin with a sod roof. As Kimberly's eyes riveted on the aging structure, her breath caught in her throat. "That's Nathan's cabin, isn't it?" she whispered, pointing with a shaky finger.

"Sure is." Eric nodded as he helped David with their bags. "My sister is cleaning it in case you'd like to use it as a honeymoon cabin. I phoned to tell her and my father you were coming. Sorry it's not in the best repair, but if you wish to use it, at least it's more private. There's no plumbing or electricity, but we have lanterns, and there's an outhouse behind it. You're more than welcome to use our bathroom and shower though. If you'd prefer to stay in the big cabin the lights work off a generator and it's comfortable and modern. We can put you up in my room, and I'll sleep in the loft."

"No thanks, the cabin will be great," David said, nodding at

Kimberly who was hurrying toward it. "My wife is so excited, a tent would suffice."

Inside the cabin, Kimberly studied the home Nathan had built for Marnie nearly a century ago. The rustic table, two chairs, a wash stand, and corner shelves were all hand hewn. A double bed with high log posts was hand carved with crude yet beautiful designs reflecting Indian artistry. In another far corner were a cleverly constructed rocking chair and a log cradle. As Kimberly looked about, she could see signs every-where of Nathan's love for Marnie. She felt an overwhelming sense of appreciation for this humble hard-working man her great-grandfather had deemed as worthless.

Kimberly brushed a tear from her eye and turned away as Eric and David entered the single room with their luggage. A moment later, Rachel came in with fresh bedding and Eric introduced her to his guests.

Rachel's skin was more golden brown than Eric's. Her hair glistened like black silk hanging just below her waist. Unlike her brother's black eyes, hers were a soft hazel green. She smiled, showing straight white teeth as she shook hands with David and Kimberly. Her welcome to them was timid but warm, and she quickly excused herself to make the bed. Kimberly offered to help, while Eric took David to the house to meet his father, Sam Duncan.

After supper, Kimberly and David returned to the cabin, feeling the strain of their long day. They retired early and David was soon snoring softly.

The cabin was dark as shadows from the trees blocked the twilight in this far northern land, where the deepening August sunset still never darkened the sky. Kimberly lay in the stillness looking out the only window at a few faint stars and an enor-mous moon peeking over the tops of the trees.

When she snuggled more deeply under the comforter, unusual warmth filled the room. As it surrounded her, Kimberly felt like she was sinking into the soft mattress. Then a whisper broke the silence. "Basi sechoya, no'ideyo."

Kimberly sat upright, expecting to see someone in the

shadows, but she and David were alone. Yet the warmth remained close, a presence that was somehow familiar. She nudged David awake. "I heard the voice again, David," she whispered. "It was the same words I heard before." She paused as a wave of understanding began to unfold. "Honey, I think a lot more is happening here than just helping to find Nathan's gold mine. I feel an awesome power or influence brought us here. I sense we're involved in a sacred mission of some kind."

David raised up, propping himself against the headboard. Kimberly cuddled against him, laying her head on his shoulder. "Can you feel it David? There's a peace in here that makes me tingle to my toes."

"Yes Kimmy, I feel it," he whispered.

Early the next morning, David awoke and crawled out of bed. It was cold in the cabin, and he wanted to start a fire in the primitive Yukon stove so it would be warm when Kimberly woke up. Still sleepy and unsteady, he tripped over a suitcase. Staggering to catch his balance, his right foot landed hard against the wooden floor. The aging plank splintered and gave way, throwing him to the floor as his foot went through the hole. "Ow!" he cried as the jolt shot through his leg and the splintered wood scraped his ankle.

Kimberly bolted upright in bed. "David, what happened? Are you hurt?" She quickly found her way to the table and lit the lamp.

"No, just a little scrape," David said pulling his foot back through the hole. His toe caught on something cold, knocking it into the opening. "There's something under here," David said, breaking away the splintered wood. He reached beneath the floor and withdrew a rusty metal box.

Kimberly's heart pounded. "Hurry, open it!"

David brushed away some of the thick dust, then pried against the lid with his pocket knife. The lid fell open. Staring at the contents, David and Kimberly were astonished. In the top of the lid was a smaller copy of the picture of Marnie and Nathan that David had discovered in Marnie's trunk. An aged mining claim notice lay on top of a diary. David picked up the diary and opened the front cover. Scrawled in faded ink were the words: "Memoirs of Nathan Demeron."

"David, look," Kimberly whispered, gazing at the remaining contents of the box. There was a pile of old letters bound together by rawhide string. Lifting them from the rusty metal that had preserved them, Kimberly choked out the words; "They're all from great Aunt Marnie."

The dry and brittle rawhide broke, dumping the letters onto the floor. A small rolled paper tied with faded ribbon fell separate from the letters. As David picked up the letters, Kimberly untied the ribbon and carefully unrolled the paper. Suddenly, she gasped, sitting down hard on the floor as she lost her balance.

"What is it Kim?" David asked, seeing the look of shock on his wife's face.

"They were married," she whispered. "They must have done it in secret. This is their marriage certificate, and the photograph has to be their wedding picture."

The weather was dreary with pouring rain, so David and Kimberly started a cozy fire. Then they snuggled together on the bed to examine their treasures.

David scanned through the diary while Kimberly read letters filled with pain and sweet expressions of love from her great-aunt. For so many years, Marnie had been lost to her family. Now, Kimberly read with eagerness and compassion as Marnie became known and beloved to her. As each letter drew them closer, Kimberly became increasingly aware that the bond between Marnie and herself had always been there.

"Listen to this," David said, bringing Kimberly back. She rested her head on David's chest as he read the beginning excerpt from the diary.

"My dearest beloved Marnie; today I have decided to address each journal entry to you. That way, I can feel you are near as I record my adventures, and this terrible loneliness may not seem so unbearable. My first diary was lost, and it has been some months since I have been able to write as I have been very ill. I have now

acquired a new diary, thus I will start at the beginning and bring you up to date. I will not be writing these things in my letters to you, as they are records of my hardships. Life threatening trials I've suffered in this wild and treacherous land where white men have become my enemies and the uncivilized Indians have become my dearest friends.

"You, my beloved wife, already carry too much grief and I would never grieve you further by letting you know how much I have endured here.

"After the torturous climb up the 'Chilkoot Trail,' and the long and bitter journey to the Klondike, I arrived too late, and the good mining ground was all claimed. By then, I was destitute. I took up working for a successful miner, but the work was hard and paid little. He was a harsh man, but he was fair, and when he no longer needed me, he gave me a small bag of gold dust as payment, and told me gold had been discovered at a place near Circle City far down the Yukon River. I purchased some mining gear, but lacked enough gold to travel by steamer. I happened on some fellows who were taking a raft down the mighty Yukon. They said they could take me on. It was well into autumn, and the days were cold and often stormy, but my love for you drove me on. I was certain that through faith and hope, God would lead me, answering my prayers so you and I can be together forever.

"One night, I awoke to find one of the fellows going through my gear. He had discovered my gold, and brotherhood was a forgotten virtue. As I confronted him, I was struck from behind by a terrible blow that rendered me unconscious. Then I was thrown into the icy waters of the Yukon to drown.

"In his mercy, God had provided a savior for me. A young Athabaskan Indian had traded furs at a white settlement and was returning to his people's trapping camp on the edge of a place called Menhti. He had moved his canoe into the willows to wait as our raft passed. This country grows darker this time of year, and a man sees fewer hours of daylight, but the nights are beautiful. There is a wondrous magic here called "yoyekoyh," when beautiful colors play and dance in the sky and the moon grows huge. When the men cast me adrift, my friend heard the splash. In the bright glow of the moon and the northern lights, he saw the silty water dragging me under. He pulled me into his canoe and covered me with blankets he had traded for. Then he searched for a place to camp.

"When I awakened, my new friend, Yuzri Tso' had dried me and dressed me in some of his caribou skins. I was sick and dizzy many days, hardly able to eat, and I had caught such a chill from the river, that I shook until I thought my bones would break. Yuzri Tso' called me Dedezis, which I later learned means "he is shivering." For a week, we continued our journey down the Yukon, then up the Tanana to the Tolovana River and on to the Indian camp.

"I believe I was nearly dead by then, as I recall nothing for several more weeks. Yuzri Tso' and his wife Kalt'oddha, nursed me back to health. My friend speaks some English, and he is teaching me his native tongue, so I am finally not alone. They are letting me stay with them through the long dark winter, and I am well cared for. My dear Marnie, I see God's hand in my rescue by these good people. As the murky waters of the Yukon were about to swallow me forever, Yuzri Tso' (who's name in English means "they call his name beaver") pulled me from the water, and Kalt'oddha was the lovely flower of the waters who cared for me. God sent a beaver and a water lily to save me.

"Yuzri Tso' is against mining the earth for gold. He says it's bad medicine. He doesn't trust whites. Too many times his people have suffered untold hardships when the white men came in floods to find gold. For some reason he trusts me though, and understands my predicament. When the winter is over, he will take me to a place I have promised to keep secret. There, my beloved Marnie is my gold, and our future.

"Dearest, I can only imagine how joyous it will be to hold you again in my arms and look into your beautiful face. I dream and pray for that day with all my heart. Until the next time I write, farewell my precious wife."

David and Kimberly continued to study the diary and letters. They politely refused breakfast, unable to pull themselves from the intriguing history they had discovered.

Suddenly, Kimberly dropped a letter she was reading with

a startled cry of disbelief. Her eyes darted to the cradle in the far corner, then back to the letter in her lap.

"What's wrong, Kim?" David asked as she gasped for the breath that astonishment had sucked from her.

She picked the letter up again with shaking fingers, unable to control the tears as she read on, leaving David confused and concerned. Finally, her hand dropped to her side, the letter loose in her fingers. She turned to David, bathing his chest with tears.

Wondering what tragic mystery had made her cry, he held her until her sobs had ebbed. "Honey? What is it?"

She sat up, drying her eyes on the sheet. She took a shaky breath and spoke in hushed tones. "No wonder Marnie has always been close to me."

"What?" David asked.

"Oh David, it's hard to believe that Jacob and Martha Slater could have perpetrated such a bizarre deception against their own daughter! She suffered so much it breaks my heart. Marnie didn't realize she was pregnant when Nathan left for Alaska. Of course her father didn't know she was married. When he found out about the baby, he was insane with anger, and he beat her. She almost lost the baby. She told her father she was married, but he refused to believe her. He forced her into seclusion. Then when the baby was born, he forced her to give the baby to her mother who had faked pregnancy so the Slater name would not be shamed.

"Marnie had planned to steal their baby and run away with Nathan when he returned from Alaska." Kimberly paused, giving a long sigh. "We know the rest of the story." She wiped her eyes again, handing David the letter. "David, her baby was my grandfather, Donald. Marnie wasn't my aunt, she was my great-grandmother, and Nathan Demeron was my great-grandfather!"

Chapter 33

At lunch, Kimberly sat beside Rachel and touched her hand. "Do you speak your native language?" she asked. Rachel nodded.

"Basi sechoya no'ideyo . . . do you know what that means?"

Rachel looked surprised. "Yes, it says *thank you my grandchild, you have come.* Where did you hear these words?"

"They have come to my mind many times in the past week." Kimberly's voice was barely audible. She sighed, leaning back in the chair. *All these years it's been my grandfather who's been pulling my heart here,* she thought, feeling a sense of understanding and fulfillment she had never before known. *I had to come. He and Grandmother Marnie wanted me to know the truth.*

Kimberly watched raindrops forming tiny trails down the window of the main house. "It's something I discovered today. I can't explain right now, Roxanne," Kimberly said, running her fingers across the picture of her great-grandparents. "There's just too much to tell, and reception on this cell phone isn't the greatest. Please come as soon as possible. Bring Jerry if he can break away from his shop. We need all the help we can get."

The weather had cleared two days later when Jerry and Roxanne arrived. Eric, David, and Kimberly ran to meet the helicopter. Roxanne appeared first, her brown eyes dancing with excitement as she stepped down. She flashed her usual friendly smile, extending her hand in introduction to Eric.

Kimberly completed the introductions. Eric nodded and took Roxy's hand, then Jerry's. Then he excused himself to help with the luggage.

Roxanne turned and embraced Kimberly. "Now stop torturing me, Kim. What's this all about? I'm dying of curiosity."

"I'll tell you," Kimberly promised. "But I think we'd better get you settled first."

Jerry and David clasped hands, talking at the same time. "You go first," David said, laughing as he helped Jerry and Eric with the luggage.

Jerry grinned. "I've crashed parties before, but this is the first time I've ever crashed a honeymoon. "What's up that's so all-fired important?"

"We'll tell you at lunch," David answered. "Who's watching the gallery?"

"Sally's been planning a change in her work and location. I used my brotherly influence to convince her that now is a good time to give Slatersville a try. She's keeping shop while she looks over the area. Since my big deal with the hotel chain is in the bag, I was free to get away."

At the main house, more introductions were made. Rachel showed Roxanne to a cot in her room, and Jerry moved his bags to the loft.

When the new guests were settled, everyone assembled for lunch. As David took a seat beside Roxanne, he noticed her left hand. "What's this?" he asked, lifting her hand and thrusting the diamond ring on her finger into Jerry's face.

Jerry pushed his glasses up on his nose. "Well, what does it look like?" he asked, grinning proudly at Roxanne, who flushed a slight pink beneath her blond curls. "The date's set for December twenty-fourth. We wanted each other for Christmas."

As cheerful congratulations went around the table, Eric's dark eyes met with Roxanne's, and then he quickly glanced away.

"Okay, you know our news," Roxanne said. "What's yours?"

Kimberly grew serious. "You'd better brace yourself Roxy, this is a bombshell." She took a deep breath, and then continued. "Your rightful name is not Roxanne Slater, it's Roxanne Demeron."

"What are you talking about?" Roxanne asked as confusion filled her eyes.

"It's true," David said. "This claim the Duncan's are working belonged to Nathan Demeron, Marnie's husband."

"Marnie never married him," Roxanne snapped, stunned at what she was hearing.

"Yes, she did." Kimberly handed Roxanne the marriage certificate.

Roxanne unrolled the paper and took a quick breath. The confusion on her face grew deeper. "So, what does that have to do with my name?"

Kimberly reached across David, placing her hand on her cousin's hand. "Donald wasn't Marnie's brother, Roxy. He was her son." Kimberly felt Roxanne's muscles flinch under her hand as the color drained from her face. "I know it's a shock," Kimberly said. "All these years, we believed Grandpa was a Slater, now we discover that it was a lie and we aren't who we thought we were. Marnie and Nathan are our real great-grand-parents, and the name Demeron is our true identity."

Roxanne sat in a stupor. Finally she excused herself and slipped into the bedroom. Jerry, who had been staring with his mouth open, started to get up.

"I'll go, Jerry," Kimberly said rising from her chair. "She probably needs family right now."

"Wow, what a revelation," Jerry said, sitting back down. "How did you find out all of this?"

"We found the information in some old letters and a journal," David answered.

Jerry had an afterthought. "For that matter, how did you even find this place? Its miles away from your planned trip, and I must say a most unusual setting for a honeymoon."

"It's a long, incredible story," David said. "I'll tell you some-time. Right now, our focus is finding a vein of gold in a cave so Mr. Duncan doesn't lose his claim. We're hoping you and Roxy can help in the search."

Jerry was dumfounded. "We came here to look for gold? What the heck do any of us know about gold mining?" Jerry shook his head. "I've always been the impulsive one, but you've got one up on me this time, Dave."

"Tell me about it." David chuckled. "Dad and I always enjoyed spelunking, but I wonder what he'd say about me searching for a cave of gold on my honeymoon."

"He'd probably tell you how mixed up you are. That's supposed to be a pot of gold somewhere near a rainbow that leads to happily ever after."

"Only in fairytales, Jerry." David laughed. "When does life ever go with the plan?"

When Kimberly and a calmer Roxanne returned, Eric placed a map in the center of the table. They studied the map and listened to Sam repeat the old Indian story about the lost mine.

Early the next morning, Eric and Rachel loaded backpacks. Then, dressed in layered clothing for unexpected changes common in the weather, the group bid Sam goodbye.

The middle-aged man, looking care-worn and tired, stood in the doorway supporting his arm cast. He smiled gratefully, then returned to his chair and sat back with a sigh.

The prospectors walked single file along a muddy moose trail, slapping at biting flies and mosquitoes. They laughed and sang as they tried to keep their balance on the slippery ground. Eric and Rachel's guests quickly adjusted to their surroundings. After all, how many tourists get to experience a real-life Alaskan adventure? Jerry and Roxanne were the life of the party, making sure there was enough noise to keep the bears away. The deep narrow trail continued through impenetrable stands of scrubby black spruce until it finally reached Brooks Creek.

Kimberly and Roxanne, muddy and rumpled, sat on the ground laughing at each other, while Rachel and the men approached a shed near the creek bank.

"We should probably have a man in each canoe in case of trouble where his strength might be needed." Eric said as he unlocked the shed. "Who knows how to handle a canoe besides Rachel and myself?"

"I usually capsized mine at scout camp," Jerry said with a grin as he and David helped drag the canoes to the bank. "David knows how to make them hum through the water though."

"Okay, you'd better go with Rachel, Jerry. I can take Roxanne with me. David and Kimberly can take the third canoe. The creek is narrow, but don't let it fool you. It's swift and deep, so be careful." Soon the canoes were ready to board.

"All we know for certain is that the cave Nathan found is somewhere along the fault line that follows the creek at the base of Tolovana Dome," Eric said pointing out features of the terrain as he spoke. "During an earthquake, the bed of the creek which is on the fault, broke away and plunged downward in relation to the mountainside while the opposite bank pushed upward, forming a steep scarp. We still have occasional tremors here, so the continual ground shifting could have totally buried the cave and Nathan's description may be useless. I wish we had more to go on. Just carefully study the up-thrust side of the scarp line for any indications of hollows or openings.

"We'll separate and scan different areas all along the claim. David, you and Kimberly take the middle section, starting from this marker to the next bandanna I will place farther upstream," he said tying a red bandanna on a branch near the bank. "The terrain can be very dangerous, and there are bears, so except for potty stops, stay in the canoe. If you find anything promising, tie one of these rags on a bush near the bank.

"Rachel and I will work either end of the claim since we know the boundaries." He paused before adding; "I want to thank all of you. I know you're making a sacrifice to help us. I hope this will prove to be worth your time."

Eric helped Roxanne into his canoe and pointed it upstream, paddling hard against the current. David and Kimberly followed Eric, working to keep their canoe stable in the swift stream.

Jerry thrust his paddle into the water, feeling rather clumsy. He tried to match Rachel's strokes as she maintained a slower drift against the force of the downstream current.

She smiled. "You are doing well, Jerry. Just keep us from bumping the shoreline." Her voice was timid, but she made certain he could hear her above the mild rush of the water. Rachel disembarked time and again to check out possibilities along the shoreline. The foliage was dense and the ground rugged, but it was obvious she knew her task and how to perform it. Jerry, on the other hand, had strong doubts that he would be of any help at all. He didn't even know what to look for.

About noon, Rachel paddled toward the shore along an open strip of ground. "We will stretch our legs and eat here," she said, stepping onto the shore. Jerry moved out of the canoe as Rachel steadied it.

He strolled toward the crowded black spruce to work out some cramped muscles. "Do not go out there, Jerry," Rachel warned, catching his arm. "This permafrost looks solid, but some places are thawed. It can be very unstable. There are many bogs covered with only a dry layer of moss that will give way underfoot and swallow a man in twenty or thirty feet of black muck. Besides, if you go into the trees, the mosquitoes will devour you for lunch. Go behind that big rock if you need privacy."

"Sounds pretty mean. Thanks for the warning," he said with a grin.

Jerry studied the expression in Rachel's hazel green eyes, admiring the beauty of this shy young Indian woman who seemed so delicate, yet so in control of a savage land. As they ate their lunch, Jerry couldn't resist the urge to force conversation from his partner by asking her question after question. He delighted in listening to her native accent. He was impressed by her knowledge, experience, and her love and respect for her wild environment. He found her to be devoted to her family, dedicated to her profession, and determined to preserve the values of her native people.

Back in the canoe, Jerry scanned the fault scarp, wondering what subjects Eric and Roxy had discussed during lunch. He smiled to himself, thinking how lucky he was to have found a girl like Roxanne.

The week advanced, but the prospectors had no success. Each evening they pulled their canoes ashore and hiked back home. They enjoyed a campfire built in a stone lined pit, and some wonderful Indian dishes prepared over the flames or buried in the ashes. They shared stories and traditions, and they ate lots of s'mores. Each morning as twilight began to lift they hiked back to the canoes to begin the search again.

Chapter 34

On Sunday the group took a welcome break. Attending church was out of the question due to the remoteness, so David and Kimberly spent a restful day reading scriptures, conversing with their friends, and sharing Marnie's letters and Nathan's journal with Roxanne and Jerry.

That evening, Rachel was reading to Sam in the main cabin. Eric went for a walk, and Roxanne said she had a headache and wanted to retire early. Jerry strolled to the little cabin with Kimberly and David. He visited for a while, then said good night, and walked back toward the main house. Suddenly, he froze as soft voices from the twilight shadows reached his ears.

Deciding to prepare for bed as well, David took his toothbrush and followed Jerry toward the main house. Seeing his friend in the path ahead, he was about to speak when he also heard voices and stopped dead still. It was Roxanne and her words made David's blood run hot, yet he was too stunned to move.

"I think I love you too, Eric. I don't know . . . this has all happened so fast. I adore Jerry, though. I can't bear to hurt him like this."

"We have to tell him Roxanne, whatever the cost. I didn't mean for this to happen either, but it has. It wouldn't be fair to him or to us to ignore it and just return to our own lives." Eric and Roxanne moved out of the shadows as they strolled hand in hand. Eric paused, taking her in his arms. "I've never met anyone like you before. You are like music in the wind, laughter of the waters, and your spirit bears the gentleness of a fawn. I don't want to lose you." As their lips met, David saw Jerry back away, and lean weakly against a tree.

Jerry's slumped and broken form was too much for David. The anger in him exploded as he threw himself at Eric. "You snake!" he bellowed. "You lying dirty . . ." he struck hard with his fist, knocking Eric to the ground. Roxanne jumped back with a startled shriek.

Kimberly burst out of the cabin door as David charged toward Eric, ready to deliver another blow. "David!" she cried. Her voice stopped him for a moment, giving her time to grab his arm. "What's going on?'

Hearing the commotion, Rachel rushed from the house and ran toward her brother.

Roxanne dropped to her knees beside Eric as he shook his head and raised up on one elbow. Then she noticed Jerry and caught a glimpse of his agonized face. "Oh Jerry, I'm so sorry. I didn't want you to find out like this." She started to cry.

Jerry had watched the nightmarish spectacle in dazed shock. Now Roxanne's tears brought him back to a harsh cold reality. He had lost her. He looked at her with an empty stare, then ran into the darkness of the trees.

David jerked his arm free from Kimberly's grasp and ran after Jerry.

Furious at her brother's betrayal of those who had been so willing to help, Rachel grabbed a survival kit and followed the clumsy trail Jerry and David had left. She knew death was common among travelers who dared venture through the dense forests. The dangers were even more threatening for Jerry and David, who were driven by blind emotion through the dusky light. After pushing at a rapid pace for almost two hours, there was still no sign of the men. "Jerry! David!" Rachel called again and again, listening to the sounds of the forest as she began to fear the worst.

"Over here," came a strained reply. She forced her way through a heavy wall of spruce and willows and saw David sitting with his back against a tree, gasping for breath.

"I couldn't catch him," he panted, ignoring the blood seeping from scratches on his arms and face. "He's crazy with grief. He's just had too much hurt."

"You must rest, David," Rachel said placing her hand gently on his shoulder. "Stay here. I will find Jerry."

He nodded, laying his elbows on his knees. He shook his head, burying his face in his hands.

With tears stinging his eyes, Jerry ran wildly away from pain and despair. He heard David's voice calling, but David couldn't help now. It was too late. Pushing through nearly impassable foliage, Jerry's reasoning powers were gone. He just wanted to get far away. The agony of Roxanne's kiss on Eric's lips haunted him with every step. Sharp branches ripped at him, but nothing hurt, only the unbearable pain in his heart.

Suddenly, as he reached a clearing, he tripped over a log, knocking off his glasses. His foot caught in the crook of a branch. He felt an agonizing snap in his thigh as his body twisted and he plunged through the thin mossy layer covering a bog. The rank-smelling ooze surrounded him, the chilling slime jolting him to his senses. For a moment, pain was replaced by panic. Jerry cried out, struggling against the pull of the bog, but he only sank deeper. He stopped struggling and looked for something he could grasp onto. A small birch tree near his arm offered hope. He strained to touch its trunk, but it was just out of reach. He felt himself sinking deeper. He was helpless.

Was this what death was like . . . just silent acceptance of the inevitable? The searing pain in his thigh brought back an awareness of sharper pain in his heart. "Oh, Roxanne," he cried. "I loved you so much." The slime climbed higher on his shoulders. Soon, his suffering would disappear into the blackness of the muck and he wouldn't ever hurt again.

His mind swept to the past, his memories more clear and vivid than they had ever been. Suddenly, Jerry realized he didn't hate his father anymore. A light of understanding clicked on in his mind like a lamp switch. This was what his father had felt like, the pain too intolerable, himself too weak, too much a failure to care anymore.

Jerry stopped straining to reach the tree and sighed as his arm fell limply into the muck. He could see his father's face, the final look of defeat, and the terrible sadness. As the memory engulfed him, Jerry realized he didn't care anymore either. He was just too sick and tired to care. All he wanted now was for this rotten painful existence to be gone forever.

Jerry moaned and laid his head back into the cold dank comfort of the bog, willing the muck to swallow his pain and grief, willing it to devour him into its sticky putrid belly along with the moose, and caribou, and mastodons it had been swallowing for centuries. Jerry took one long last look at the gray sky and closed his eyes.

"No," something inside him screamed. "Not this way! You have to try!" Jerry raised his head for a moment, but he was too weak and discouraged to respond. He again rested his head in the muck, giving his life to his black oozing grave.

Chapter 35

"Jerry," Rachel's cry momentarily roused him as she broke through the brush and halted in mid-step. "Oh dear God, help me," she prayed.

"Jerry, do not move until I can find something to reach you with." She looked about, grabbing a long branch broken off a tree by the recent storm. Throwing herself on her stomach, she pushed the branch toward Jerry's hand. "Grab the branch, Jerry," she cried. Jerry didn't respond. "Jerry, look at me! Take hold of the branch!" He remained motionless, his eyes closed.

"David!" Rachel screamed, praying he could hear her. "David, help!"

Desperate to save him, Rachel jammed the sharp point of the branch against Jerry's hand. He stirred and moaned, but only sank deeper. "David!" she screamed again. "Jerry, wake up!" she cried, jabbing harder with the branch. He groaned and raised his head.

"Rachel, where are you?" David's voice was drawing near.

"I am over here. Hurry! I am losing him!"

David burst through the thick trees and froze, his breath leaving him in a horrified gasp.

"Jerry, please!" Rachel's plea was frantic as she pushed her shoulders beyond the soggy edge of the bog, ramming the branch into his arm. He winced and groaned, his head drooping forward.

David sprang into action, casting a small stone into the muck a fraction of an inch from Jerry's head. The cold slime splashed Jerry's face, and he roused a little. "Jerry!" David commanded. "Snap out of it! Grab hold of that branch!" He pelted Jerry's face with another gooey splash. Jerry opened his glassy eyes and gradually focused on David. Desperate to trigger Jerry's adrenaline, David splashed him with another rock and bellowed. "You're a coward, Jerry. If you don't grab that branch, you're a coward just like your old man was!" David pelted another rock beneath Jerry's chin, splattering the muck into a corner of Jerry's mouth. Jerry sputtered and glared at David, then slowly reached out and grasped the branch with his hand.

It took all of David and Rachel's strength to ease Jerry's body from the thick muck. Whenever Jerry weakened or started to slip away, David plastered him with another splash in his face, taunting him until he saw a spark of fire in Jerry's eyes.

Finally they all lay exhausted on solid ground. Whispering a heartfelt prayer of gratitude over, and over, and over, David wrapped Jerry's shivering body in his arms and held him close.

As soon as Rachel caught her breath, she gathered some dry twigs and branches from beneath a heavy clump of spruce trees and started a fire. She pulled a mat and space blanket from her survival pack and laid them out for Jerry, then placed the pack beside David and went to get help.

David's hands were shaking as he tried to remove Jerry's wet clothes. Fumbling clumsily with the shirt buttons, he became exasperated and finally ripped the shirt open. Jerry was shivering, his teeth chattering violently. He was semiconscious as David worked frantically to undress him. He winced or moaned whenever he was moved, and David soon discovered the broken thigh. He covered his injured friend with the blanket, then made a splint with a small spruce trunk, his handkerchief, and Jerry's belt. After carefully moving Jerry onto the mat, he bundled the blanket around his stricken brother.

David shuddered as he wiped the muck from Jerry's face with gauze pads, trying to quell the inconceivable thought that haunted him; the hideous vision of Jerry struggling for breath beneath the bog while slimy black goo filled his lungs. He attempted to block the terrifying image from his mind by talking. He didn't know what he said, he just talked. Jerry was still shivering uncontrollably. He was pale and his lips were blue. David worked to increase Jerry's body temperature by rubbing his arms and other leg through the blanket.

Finally, Jerry roused a little and watched David silently with piercing eyes.

David forced a worried grin. "Guess it's my turn to fret about you," he said tucking the blanket more tightly around Jerry's shoulders.

Jerry's glare was penetrating. "I'm not a coward," he mumbled through chattering teeth, then turned his face away.

David swallowed hard, choking down the lump in his throat. "I know, Jerry," he said, gripping his friend's shoulder. "You're one of the bravest men I've ever known." David sniffed, wiping his eyes on his shirttail. Remembering the magnitude of Jerry's suffering through the years, David wondered why he hadn't better understood his friend's agony. He had never imagined suicide to be an option. He shuddered, shaking his head then continued to watch over his friend with grave concern as he waited for help.

Nearly three hours later, a helicopter finally settled on the far side of the clearing. Rachel and the paramedics hurried to Jerry's side. "How is he?" she asked, kneeling next to Jerry as the paramedics opened their cases.

Jerry caught her hand in his. "I'll survive," he mumbled, "thanks to you."

She smiled and squeezed his hand, then moved back so the paramedics could help him.

"We'll take him to the hospital in Fairbanks," the EMT told David as the pilot set down at the claim to let Rachel and David out. "Sorry we can't take you with us."

"I'll be okay," Jerry said, mustering a weak smile through a grimace of pain as he released David's hand.

Kimberly was anxiously waiting when David stepped out of the helicopter. "How's Jerry?" she asked, her eyes full of worry and sadness.

David glared at her. "Not good. A fractured femur and severe hypothermia, not to mention his wrecked mental state. He nearly died thanks to your despicable cousin."

David turned to Rachel and embraced her, trying to keep his emotions in check before he spoke. "Thanks for saving both our skins out there," he said. "You were an angel of mercy. It's almost morning. You'd better get some rest." Feeling heavy-hearted and weak from strain, David walked to the cabin on shaky legs, leaving Kimberly staring after him.

Kimberly entered the cabin as David was stripping off his mucky clothes. She watched silently as he washed up in the basin and crawled into bed.

"Where's that black-eyed Casanova and your two-timing cousin?" David asked curtly.

"They left by canoe to catch a float plane to Kodiak. They figured staying here would only make things worse."

"Well, so much for his dad's health and security. See a pretty face, and scruples become dog meat, no matter who gets hurt. Let's pack up and get out of here tomorrow."

"Honey, I'm so sorry. I feel terrible about all of this," Kimberly said, touching David's shoulder. "I wish I could help."

David jerked away from her hand and turned toward the wall. "Just go away and leave me alone."

Kimberly was taken back by David's hostility. Why was he taking his anger out on her? Was he so blind in his bitterness that he couldn't see she was as shaken and worried about Jerry as he was? Kimberly was furious at Roxanne too, but she was also worried about her cousin. She'd never seen Roxy so down. Feeling the weight of sorrow, Kimberly walked alone among the tall white spruce behind the house, wishing the nightmare into oblivion. Fate had set a new stage and all the wishing in the world couldn't make things as they had been. Kimberly sat on the permafrost, hugging her knees. Then she laid her head on her arms and cried.

When she could compose herself, Kimberly called the hospital to check on Jerry. She was relieved to hear that he had improved and was now listed in satisfactory condition.

David slept the heavy sleep of mental and physical exhaustion most of the day. When he woke up, he was still sharp-tongued and distant toward Kimberly. She brought him supper, but he coldly refused. Kimberly hadn't slept at all, and her patience was wearing thin.

"David, I've had all I'm going to take from you," she slammed the dinner tray onto the table. "I didn't cause any of this; I didn't make it happen, and I'm not accountable for my cousin's sins. Until you can speak to me with a civil tongue, I'll be staying with Rachel." She stormed out, leaving David staring after her.

David spent a restless night alone, still haunted by the image of his friend slipping beneath the cold black surface of the bog. Over and over, the hideous death Jerry nearly suffered tortured David. He shuddered. *How could I have been so blind not to see that kind of treachery in Roxanne?* He thought, I should have sensed it and warned Jerry. *How could Kimberly have been so reckless with Jerry's soul? Hadn't he been hurt enough for a lifetime? Kimberly knew Roxanne better than anyone. She never should have introduced him to such a witch.* David's anger continued to mount as he tossed about on the bed. Finally, he got up and began pacing around the patched hole in the cabin floor.

Suddenly he stopped, sick with shame and guilt. It wasn't Kimberly's doing. He knew that. She would never hurt Jerry. Why had he faulted her? He had been so harsh and cold toward his wife, giving his anger control of his senses. Yet the nightmare repeating itself over and over in his mind only rekindled the anger in him like a fire raging against the winds of reason. What could the future hold for Jerry now?

He realized he had to come to peace within himself before he could put things right with Kimberly. He took a deep breath then knelt by the bed humbly pleading for divine healing of his anger. He remained on his knees for a long time.

Finally, in the early morning hours, David approached the large cabin and tapped on Rachel's door. She led him to Kimberly. He sat on the cot beside his wife, smoothing her hair. Kimberly opened her eyes as David kissed her forehead. "Honey, I'm sorry. I've been a total jerk." He hung his head.

"Please come back to the cabin, and we'll talk."

"I have no excuse for the way I acted, Kim. I've been so overwrought and angry, all I wanted to do was hit someone," he said as they sat at Nathan's table. "I had no right to take it out on you. I just . . . I never felt more scared or helpless in my life. Jerry's my brother and I almost lost him."

"I know," Kimberly answered. "Rachel told me what happened. It must have been terrifying beyond belief. I do understand your anger, David, but you need to realize that you're not alone in this. I'm as hurt and upset as you are. Jerry's very special to me. I feel his pain, and I'm heartbroken for him." She ran her fingers across David's cheek. "More than anything in the world, I wish that I could undo what's been done . . . We can pray for him, though, Honey. That we can do." David nodded, taking Kimberly's hands in his.

In the flickering light of the lantern, two figures knelt with bowed heads, petitioning the great God of love to comfort and heal a beloved friend. Finally they rose to their feet and embraced, then retired to await the full light of day.

Chapter 36

Kimberly bolted upright in bed. "David!" She shook him awake. "Honey, I know you're eager to see Jerry, but we can't leave today. We have to look for the cave one more time." Her eyes were pleading and excited.

David sat up, running his hand through his tangled hair. "Kim, there are only three of us to do what six couldn't do last week. I know it's rotten to leave Rachel alone in this mess, but . . ."

"I saw it David. I saw the cave in a dream just like Grandfather described it. I can find it. I know I can. Maybe if we hurry, we can still get to Fairbanks to see Jerry today. Please, David. We have to try."

Her plea carried sureness, a power of conviction so strong that David sensed her dream to be more than just a dream. He tossed back the covers. "All right Kim, go tell Rachel. I'll get dressed and start packing while you two get ready.

"Where the great tree leaps to the sky . . ." Kimberly said as she studied the scarp line along Brooks Creek. "The tree is still there, but its top is broken off, and its base is so overgrown with foliage that we never could have found it."

After several hours, Rachel pulled their canoe toward the bank. "We should take a break and eat."

"No," Kimberly pressed. "We need to keep looking. I'm getting goosebumps. I think we're close."

They paddled for some time. Then, as they rounded a bend in the creek, Kimberly leaped forward in the canoe. "There it is," she cried.

"Kim, sit down. You nearly capsized us," David said, trying to stabilize the canoe. As they touched shore, David caught

Kimberly's jacket sleeve and held her fast. "Hold on. Let Rachel check the bank first. The cave has been here for a hundred years. It won't disappear while we take time to play it safe."

When Rachel motioned to them, Kimberly nearly flew up the bank and began tugging on the bushes. They were frozen in the permafrost. Rachel took an ax from her pack and began chopping at the heavy growth.

"Here, let me chop while you and Kimberly clear away the brush," David said. He felled several small trees and exposed a portion of the giant tree's enormous root system, partially suspended in the air. He chopped out more bushes beneath the roots, revealing a narrow opening to a cave.

Rachel gasped, grabbing David's arm for support. Then she quickly pulled a headlamp from her pack and put it on. Handing flashlights to her partners, she could hardly contain her excitement as she crawled through the opening with David and Kimberly close behind.

Several feet inside, the tunnel opened into a cavern tall enough for them to stand upright. The cave was wide, but narrowed to about four feet in the far end. A thick layer of ice covered the rock there. Rachel flashed her light on the cave walls and moaned.

"What's wrong?" David asked.

"This does not look promising. It is country rock, fractured schist. It does not usually contain gold unless there are quartz veins." She walked around the cavern, studying the walls. David and Kimberly waited, shining their lights on the walls as though wishing hard enough might make gold suddenly appear in the rays.

Finally Rachel spoke, but her voice quivered. "This is discouraging after our long hours of searching. I will have to bring back some tools to check more closely, but I see no evidence of gold. Let us go home." She crawled back through the opening.

"Are you coming?" David asked, shining his flashlight at Kimberly. She stood toward the far end studying the ice formation. "Come on, Kim," he said. "Rachel's disappointed and hungry. We gave it all we had." He walked over, reaching for Kimberly's hand, but she pulled back. "What's wrong?"

"It doesn't make sense. If there's no gold here, why did I see this cave in my dream? You don't just dream a place you've never been."

David shrugged. "I don't know, but . . ." He looked toward the opening, then turned back to Kimberly. "Honey, I know you're disheartened, but Rachel knows a lot more than we do, and she already gave up on it. There's nothing more we can do." He reached for Kimberly's hand again.

But Kimberly stood firm. "Well, I haven't given up," she said jerking her hand away.

After the stress of the previous day, concerns about Jerry, and now the disappointment of it all for nothing but an empty cave, David felt himself growing impatient.

"Are you coming?" Rachel called.

"If I can get Kimberly unglued from this ice . . ." David never finished his sentence. From deep in the earth came a low, rumbling sound. The ground trembled as the rumbling swelled to a deafening roar.

"Earthquake," Rachel shrieked. "Get out of there."

Stumbling to maintain his balance, David grabbed Kimberly's hand, pulling her toward the opening of the cave. The earth heaved and waved under their feet, and they fell to the ground. Throwing his arms around Kimberly, David rolled under a rocky overhang just as the ceiling at the rear of the cave collapsed, exploding into boiling clouds of dust. Crouching over his wife to protect her from a shower of small rocks, David coughed, gasping for air.

"Are you all right?" Rachel cried as the ground stilled and the rumbling died away.

"Yeah, barely," David choked lifting Kimberly from the ground as she gasped for breath. "Holy cow, Kim, this obsession of yours nearly got us killed."

"David look." Kimberly's voice carried a hushed urgency.

David glanced through the swirl of settling dust where her

flashlight was pointing. "Rachel, you'd better come back in here," he called.

Above the ice wall where the ceiling had crumbled was an opening reaching far into the darkness beyond. David and Kimberly climbed over fallen rock and began removing small boulders from the entrance to another larger cave. When the hole was big enough, David carefully climbed inside, probing for loose rocks. Then he helped the women through the opening.

As Rachel shined her flashlight on the cave walls, she gave a joyous squeal. Large veins of white quartz rock containing tiny specks and threads of gold lined the walls.

"We found it!" David shouted.

Suddenly, Kimberly screamed, digging her fingernails into David's jacket sleeve. As he turned, she fell against his chest, trembling in his arms. His eyes followed the beam of her flashlight and froze on a haunting scene before him. Sitting against a rock wall dressed in tattered clothes were the yellowing bones of a human skeleton.

No one spoke for some time as David held Kimberly close. "You okay, Honey?" he finally whispered. He felt her head nod.

David approached the eerie figure, followed by the women. A chain hanging from the bib of the dusty old overalls was attached to a tarnished pocket watch. The watch was resting in the bony hand still clutched tightly by the fingers. David carefully lifted the watch from the long scrawny fingers and pried the lid open. Tucked safely inside was a picture of Marnie.

"It's Nathan," Kimberly whispered, reverently caressing the old shirtsleeve. "It's my great-grandfather." She stood in silence, staring at the remains of a man she had only heard of, but loved with a devotion that surpassed eras of time.

Rachel pointed her light at a small pile of buckskin bags. She opened the rawhide string of one and poured gold dust into the palm of her hand.

"That must be the gold Nathan was taking to Marnie," David said, stepping toward Rachel. His hand struck an old lantern, knocking it from a rocky shelf beside the skeleton. It clattered to the floor of the cave beside a crude pencil and crumbling map. David picked up the map. The worn paper flopped over his hand, revealing a scrawled message on the back.

David read the fading pencil scratches in the flashlight beam:

"My beloved Marnie, I fear I will never see you again in this life. In an effort to protect our claim and to keep my promise to Yusri Tso,' no other human knows the exact location of our mine. As I came here to get gold for the journey to bring you and Donald home, I was trapped inside by an earthquake. I have tried in vain to free myself, but there is no escape.

"I do not understand why this has happened when I long for you both so much, but I will trust myself and you, my beloved family, into the hands of God. We must lean on his tender mercies to sustain us all, in life or in death. I leave my love and prayers with you and I am at peace in my heart.

"Be not fearful of what your parents may do. God will protect our family and reunite us someday, somehow. Of this, I am as certain as I am of my undying love for you.

Forever, your devoted husband, Nathan."

Chapter 37

The rays of the Northern Lights dancing in brilliant colors across the night sky seemed to be Alaska's farewell to David and Kimberly. The helicopter would arrive in the morning to take them and the remains of Nathan Demeron back to Fairbanks. Then they would be flying home. After the coroner and deputies had removed Nathan's bones from the cave, they had approved release of the body to his great-granddaughter. David had built a makeshift coffin from wood scraps to protect the skeleton in shipment until they could purchase a casket in Fairbanks the following day.

David and Kimberly smiled at each other and embraced beneath the exquisite beauty of the sky. Then they retired into the quiet darkness of Nathan's cabin, still in awe at the miracles they had experienced. Kimberly felt a sense of freedom from all the feelings that had pressed on her since her feet had touched the shore at Skagway.

David moved closer, gently cradling his wife in his arms. With their mission fulfilled, they once again belonged to each other. Their kiss was warm and deep. They were on their honeymoon and tonight belonged to them.

The next morning as David went to the loft to pack Jerry's bags, he paused at the sound of voices below him. Rachel and her father's conversation touched his ears with a startling revelation.

"Father, since Jack and Molly are coming back today to start operations for your new mine, can you get along without me? I want to go to Fairbanks with David and Kimberly so I can stay close to Jerry. I will find an apartment and a job at the hospital. Jerry will probably be in traction for weeks, and I do not think he should be alone. David and Kimberly cannot stay. David's mother is moving into his cabin this week, and Kimberly has her grandfather's burial to attend to. I think we owe Jerry that much."

David heard Sam rise from his chair and walk over to Rachel. From his position at the top of the stairs, David could see them now. Sam put his good arm around his daughter's shoulder.

"Owing Jerry a debt isn't really what's on your mind, is it Rachel?"

"I suppose not, but I cannot help feeling responsible. He has been through a terrible ordeal, and it would not have happened if he had not come to help us."

"Do you pity the man, Honey?'

"No, I feel badly, but pity is not my motivation."

"You care about him then?"

She nodded.

"Do you really know him that well?'

"Father, I know what my heart tells me. Jerry is gentle and good-hearted. He is honest, loyal, and kind. He is a pleasant man. I enjoy being around him. He encourages others to value their self-worth. He has many qualities of great value." Rachel turned toward her father and placed her hand on his cheek. "Jerry has physical injuries that will heal . . . but his heart . . . it is broken. He needs someone right now. He needs a friend." She smiled. "I want to be that friend."

"Do you love him?"

"He was betrothed. I would not have let myself fall in love with him . . . but I think I could love him. I only know that I care, and I wish to be with him now."

"He's been deeply hurt, Rachel. That can make a man bitter. I don't want you to get hurt."

"Time can heal the deepest wounds, Father." She hugged her father and kissed him. "And so can love."

Jerry smiled, greeting his visitors as David, Kimberly, and

Rachel entered the hospital room. His eyes were sad, and he looked haggard and drained.

Clearing his throat to hide his emotions, David wrapped Jerry in a heartfelt embrace, grateful for his friend's life and courageous spirit. "Man, they don't have any intention of letting you escape for a while, do they?" He glanced at the traction and pretended a chuckle.

"Afraid not. I splintered the bone so badly this is the only way it can heal. Takes four to six weeks before they can cast me. Jerry forced a grin. "Dumb stunt, huh?" He choked, unable to keep up the front, and his face grew serious. "Dave, thanks for being there for me again. I . . . I love you, brother." He blinked hard as his voice broke.

"Me too," David said swallowing a lump in his throat as he gripped Jerry's hand in both of his. Kimberly and Rachel slipped out of the room, leaving the men alone.

Finally, Jerry spoke. "Did Roxy leave for Kodiak with Eric?"

A mixture of fierce anger at Roxanne and Eric, and heartbreaking compassion for Jerry, seized David for a moment. He released Jerry's hand and took a deep breath staring at his boots as he ran his hand through his hair. He regained control as he stood upright and faced Jerry. "Yes Jerry, she did. I'm sorry, bud."

Nodding his acceptance of what he already knew, Jerry fell silent and turned away. Finally, he looked at David, brushing away a tear with the back of his hand. "I'm glad it happened before we were married. That would have been harder." He nodded at David. "I'm made of tough leather, Dave. I'm all right." He looked away again, and David wondered just how tough he really was.

Jerry cleared his throat. "I understand my father now." An expression of wisdom filled his blue eyes as he faced David. "I've forgiven him for everything. My experience in that bog made a different man out of me." He shuddered. "That scared me so bad David . . . not so much the muck . . . the despair. It was so easy to give up . . . to want to die. Thank God you came when you did. There's no way Rachel could have pulled me out

184

of my mental state. I'd have just let myself slip away." He shook his head and swallowed a lump in his throat. "I'm ashamed that I put her through so much. Is she okay?"

"She's fine. In fact, since her dad's crew is returning to rebuild his mining operation, Rachel is applying for a nursing position here. She wants to be close so she can take care of you."

"You're not serious," Jerry said. "I don't want Rachel to feel responsible . . ."

David cut him off. "That's not her reason. Rachel needs a friend, Jerry. Even before all this happened, she had found one in you. She wants to be here for you. She's very determined. Kimberly assured me of that. Arguing won't change her mind, so you might as well be her friend and help her while she helps you.

Jerry was thoughtful. David felt encouraged as a spark of desire to reach out to someone else replaced some of the sadness in Jerry's eyes. David had succeeded in swaying Jerry's focus. Now, as fond as Rachel was of Jerry, David felt at peace that his lifelong friend, his brother, would be well attended by her devoted care.

That evening, Jerry's spirits seemed greatly lifted as Kimberly and David bid him a reluctant goodbye. "Mind Rachel and get well," David said, holding his friend in a long embrace. His voice quivered a little. "I feel like a traitor leaving you in this contraption after we drug you a thousand miles from home."

"Oh, shut up and quit blaming yourselves. You know I'm always game for an adventure! Besides, I could have fixed myself up like this falling off my bike at home. Give Jan a hug for me. Tell her to get her fishing gear ready. I'm taking her fishing the day I get home." Jerry's grin reminded David of the good old days.

As David and Kimberly left, David paused in the hall for a final look back. He watched as Rachel moved to Jerry's bedside, taking his hand in her smooth brown one.

Her long black hair fell across Jerry's arm like silken

threads as she leaned forward. Bowing her head in shame, Rachel spoke, her Athabaskan accent soft and comforting. "Jerry, I am sorry about Eric. He should not have taken advantage of your kindness and trust, to then betray you." She lifted her face, capturing Jerry's focus in the clear depths of her hazel-green eyes. "I am angry and ashamed that he has caused you such terrible pain and sadness." She shook her head and sighed, speaking in her native tongue. "Nedraya dhech'el edli like xwyh. Se draya dadhk'wn. Si am like sanh to warm nedraya." (Your heart it is torn. It is cold like winter. My heart it is burning. I am like summer to warm your heart.)

"What did you say?" Jerry asked.

Rachel smoothed a wrinkle in the hospital gown covering Jerry's chest. "I will tell you sometime," she answered as a tear slipped over her dark eyelashes. "I am sad for you, Jerry. I cannot heal the pain in your heart, but I want to be here for you, to be your friend, to help you anytime you need me. When your heart weeps, I will comfort you."

Jerry took a deep breath and swallowed hard, patting her hand. "It's better that it happened now rather than later, Rachel. Thanks to you and David, I still have my life." He gently brushed the tear from her cheek and smiled. "I'll be okay."

David took Kimberly's hand and hurried down the hall. He punched the elevator button several times, pacing in front of the doors, and clenched his teeth. Once inside the closed doors, David embraced Kimberly, buried his face in her hair, and cried.

Chapter 38

Kimberly, David, and Uncle Albert requested permission from the city to bury Nathan Demeron beside his wife and son in the family plot behind the Slater mansion. During the simple graveside service, David wondered what Jacob Slater was thinking. His rejected son-in-law had finally been brought home to be laid with honor and love beside the daughter Jacob had so jealously kept from him. Everything was right now. Great-grandfather Demeron had returned to Marnie and Donald as he had promised.

Kimberly smiled through her tears as the casket was lowered into the ground. After years of trying to imagine a happy ending for Marnie and Nathan, nothing could surpass the sweet contentment of this moment.

David held Kimberly close, realizing heaven was not that far away. He had been touched by divine powers and chosen to assist his beloved wife in this miraculous reunion beyond the grave. Sensing a thrill of gratitude for her happiness, he bowed his head and felt that his own father was nearer than he had ever imagined.

That afternoon, David and Kimberly drove to the airstrip to meet Jan's commuter flight. Two flight attendants lowered her wheelchair to the ground and wheeled her toward her family. Jan's smile was radiant, her arms outstretched long before she reached the gate. She cried out with joy as David lifted her from her chair and turned about in a circle with her in his arms. "Ah, my little Mama, it's so good to have you here."

She touched his face as if to make certain he was real, then hugged him tightly and kissed his cheek. "Oh, David, you look like a dream come true. I have missed you more than you can

187

ever know. Living near to you and your sweetheart will be the joy of my life."

Kimberly held back, not wanting to intrude.

"Where is my darling daughter?" Jan asked, glancing around.

Kimberly moved forward, embracing Jan in David's arms. "Welcome, Mother Young . . . welcome home. Well, almost home. We have quite a drive to Indian Valley."

Jan placed her hand under Kimberly's chin. "Good. That will give us time to visit and get better acquainted. David, this beautiful angel is truly heaven-sent. I know why God brought you here. She not only saved your life, she has made you glow with happiness." Jan pressed her soft cheek against Kimberly's, then turned to David. "Well Son, are you going to hold me all day, or are you going to get my bags and take me home?"

David settled Jan on the front seat of his Wrangler, tied her wheelchair to his bike rack, and loaded her bags in the rear. Kimberly climbed into the back seat, placing her hand on Jan's shoulder. Sensing wonderful warmth from this pretty blond lady in a pink suit, Kimberly felt Jan now belonged to her, too.

Jan responded by holding Kimberly's hand all the way home as she chatted and praised the beautiful scenery. When they reached Indian Valley, Jan couldn't contain her excitement at the first glimpse of her lovely mountain cabin. As David carried her through the house, she re-dressed each room in her mind with a woman's creative touch.

"Slow down, Mom," David chuckled. "I haven't even moved you in yet, and you've already re-decorated the entire cabin."

He carried her into the master bedroom. "It's been a long trip. I'm sure you're tired. How about a nap before supper?"

Kimberly watched with admiration as David laid his mother's frail body on the bed. He removed her shoes and straightened her lifeless legs, then covered her with the quilt. Squeezing her hand to his heart, he kissed her. "You're finally home, Mom. Your nurse will arrive by helicopter tomorrow morning, and the moving van should be here in the afternoon. We'll get you settled, and Kim and I will stay here tonight. Try to rest now . . . don't want you to overdo it."

Slipping Jan's shoes under the bed, Kimberly kissed her. "I love you, Mama Young. We're so happy to have you here."

"It's going to be so nice to have a daughter," Jan said, touching Kimberly's cheek. "I love you, too." Jan breathed a contented sigh and smiled as she closed her eyes.

David and Kimberly quietly stepped out of the bedroom and closed the door. Holding hands, they strolled to the pond below the cabin feeling joy in the fulfillment of a perfect day.

As they approached the pond, a breeze sent quivering ripples across the reflection of golden pink clouds. Suddenly, the surface calmed, bathed in brilliant light from the setting sun. The drifting clouds and rustling leaves of the trees seemed frozen on the water like a painting on silver canvas.

The vision of a beautiful woman appeared on the crystal surface, her auburn hair and white gown flowing against the stillness of the water. Marnie smiled, reaching out as she was joined by Nathan and a handsome young man Kimberly recognized as her grandfather, Donald. The beloved ancestors from another realm embraced in joyous reunion, their smiles warm with love that could only be eternal.

Spellbound and breathless, Kimberly and David watched as the transcendent beauty of the completed masterpiece lingered, painted by the wondrous hand of God. Then the vision was washed away by the gentle breeze as it pushed shimmering ripples of gold across the surface of the pond.

About the Author

Sharon Lewis Koho grew up on a small ranch near the town of Inkom, Idaho. Her beloved father died when she was five years old, and she and her siblings were reared in humble circumstances by a hard-working and courageous mother.

In her youth, Sharon discovered she could create any world she wanted to visit, or any story she wanted to be a part of by climbing high in the trees bordering her cherished ranch. Her daydreaming amid songs of birds, rustling leaves, and the babbling of the nearby creek, inspired many wonderful stories.

Sharon married Bill Koho from Nampa, Idaho in 1967. They were married thirty years until his death in 1997. She is the proud mother of six children.

Although she is a Licensed Practical Nurse by profession, she has had much more experience in creating and telling stories. Her favorite thing to do is to spend time with her children and grandchildren. She also enjoys visiting, traveling, camping, reading, writing, swimming, and any adventurous idea that pops into her head.